AN AMERICAN ALIBI

Mrs. Lillywhite Investigates
BOOK TEN

EMILY QUEEN

An American Alibi

ISBN- 978-1-953044-74-7

First Edition

Printed in the U.S.A.

Table of Contents

CHAPTER ONE

"Hey, lady, get outta the way!" shouted a cabbie, blaring his horn loudly enough to make Rosemary Lillywhite's ears ring. She stepped back onto the footway just in time to avoid a collision but not quickly enough to escape the spray of water coming off the cab's tires as it whizzed by.

Rosemary whipped her head around to glare at her brother after his unsuccessful attempt to stifle a guffaw. "It'll be your head on a platter, Frederick Woolridge, if I don't return to London in one piece. Wouldn't you have a simply grand time explaining to Mother how you allowed me to be run over on the streets of New York City?"

The cheeky inquiry sobered Frederick enough for Rosemary's satisfaction but did nothing to dry her stockings or improve her mood.

Since arriving in the city, she had been bumped into, shoved, and now hollered at and nearly run over by a cab. It wasn't only her legs and feet that were soaking wet; someone had also shaken a dripping umbrella in her face, and she'd nearly been poked in the eye by its ferrule. Apparently, it didn't rain frequently enough in New York to encourage proper umbrella etiquette—or any etiquette at all, for that matter. The steady drizzle had forced people into cabs, only adding to the already congested streets and creating nightmarish conditions for anyone unfamiliar with the city.

"Although you do realize, dear sister," Frederick retorted, "that I'd probably still manage to come up smelling of roses as far as Mother is concerned. I *am* her favorite child, after all." He ducked out of Rosemary's reach but still took an elbow to the ribs from his wife, Vera.

She smiled unapologetically at his wounded expression. "That's what you get for marrying your sister's oldest friend." The newlyweds bickered as though they'd been together for decades, which wasn't far off given the long-standing friendship between their families.

"You don't need to remind me you're the golden child," Rosemary said. "I know they appreciate the fact that you don't humiliate the family by having your name mentioned in conjunction with murder investigations."

"Except, of course, that time I was arrested for one," Frederick replied dryly, then softened. "Besides, while

Mother might prefer you to keep a low profile, Father is secretly far more proud of his little lady sleuth than he is of me." It was the first Rosemary had heard about that, and the idea pleased her enough to lift her spirits.

And really, New York wasn't so bad; she had to admit it was actually quite wonderful. On the whole, Londoners seemed to believe any building that hadn't already been standing for at least a couple hundred years ought to be left alone and allowed to do so. New Yorkers, though, were perfectly comfortable tearing down and rebuilding after no more than a handful of years. Her mother would say it was wasteful, and while she might have a point, Rosemary found herself—when she could safely look up—quite enjoying the modern art and architecture.

To her chagrin, none of her three traveling companions were interested in such things. If only Max had come along, she thought forlornly, she might have had an ally. Rosemary's handsome, charming beau (though his status as such had become shaky of late) enjoyed the hustle and bustle of London and would have been fascinated by the difference between its rhythm and that of New York. He would have followed her around the art galleries without protest, and they would have had a lovely time absorbing the culture of the city.

Unfortunately, Max had chosen to remain behind, citing work obligations she could hardly argue against.

He had recently been promoted to chief inspector and could hardly take an extended holiday so soon after accepting the position.

Particularly not when Rosemary's sleuthing had gotten him into hot water with his superiors. She tried not to think about that debacle and hoped it resolved itself by the time she returned from the States.

Of the group, only Desmond Cooper, Frederick's oldest chum, had visited New York before, and he hadn't stopped talking about his misadventures since they'd boarded the ocean liner all the way back in Southampton. Most of his ramblings had to do with Imogene Quinn, a pistol-wielding firecracker of a woman with whom he'd solved a murder—and who was also the latest object of his affections. Not only had she made a romantic impression on him, but Desmond had also raved, sycophantically, regarding Imogene's investigative prowess long enough to grate on Rosemary's nerves.

"Didn't it sound to you as though Desmond's crime-solving was down to a bit of fortunate luck?" she had asked Vera while the pair dressed for dinner. "I'm beginning to wish I had brought along one of Dash's muzzles to use on him. If I have to hear him wax lyrical any longer, I might go mad!"

Vera had thrown her head back in a throaty laugh. "Is that devil on your shoulder whispering *you're* the sleuth of the group? Suggesting that perhaps you might have solved the mystery faster or with fewer clues?"

Rosemary had wanted to protest, to insist her irritation had nothing to do with envy, but that would have been a lie. Her head knew Desmond deserved to feel proud of himself for ensuring justice was served. Her heart echoed the sentiment, but she feared Vera wasn't entirely incorrect and shook her head to dislodge the shameful thought.

"You're right. I'm acting childishly. After all, I don't hold a monopoly on catching murderers, even though it sometimes feels as though I do." The admission did nothing to lift the dark cloud over Rosemary's head.

Vera had rolled her eyes out of her friend's line of sight and swallowed the urge to comment. Instead, she waited, knowing that pressing would only prolong the inevitable.

Sure enough, after a long moment of thought, Rosemary had burst, "What more could she possibly want? Desmond's got the whole package, surely. He's handsome, kind, gentle, and funny—not to mention filthy rich."

At the crux of the matter was the state of Desmond's heart, a fact that Vera, whose deductive skills tended to be overlooked, had already discerned. "She could ask you the same question, Rosie. After all, she wouldn't have had a chance with Des if you hadn't turned him down in the first place."

Rosemary had shot Vera a look of irritation reserved for the very best of friends. "Desmond's affections aren't the trouble if that's what you're thinking," she said. "Just because I used to have a crush on him doesn't mean this is a case of if-I-can't-have-him-nobody-else-can."

"Of course, it isn't," Vera had replied. "I know you better than that. You realized you didn't love Desmond that way after one kiss, but you still don't want him to fall for someone who doesn't appreciate him. Perhaps this Imogene's reason for rejecting Desmond is just as valid as yours. Have you thought of that?"

Rosemary hadn't answered, and neither had she softened, but she was quite keen to get to dinner, and so was the man they'd been discussing—or, rather, to get dinner over with as quickly as possible.

Desmond had love—or at least infatuation—on his mind and had done nothing less than jump around like an unruly child ever since checking into their hotel. Rosemary had assumed they'd be staying in a luxury suite at The Plaza or another comparable establishment, but at Imogene's suggestion—and Desmond's insistence—they'd booked a bank of rooms at a place slightly further downtown.

Frederick's insistence they stay near the clubs didn't hurt Desmond's case. Frederick was almost as obsessed with jazz as he was with American baseball and had talked their ears off about Paul Whiteman and Babe Ruth all through dinner.

Vera, a second-generation stage actress, had secured tickets to all the on- and off-Broadway shows and had dreams of securing a film role while in New York. Then, of course, there was the shopping. Whatever time Vera had left would be devoted to scouring all the shops on Fifth Avenue for treasures to fill her many trunks. Most likely dragging Rosemary along with her.

Rosemary was the only one, it seemed, who fancied a comfortable bed and concierge service, but she'd sooner eat her own shoe than let herself be dubbed a flat tire. And so, they were booked into a set of rooms at The Roosevelt Hotel, which was of high enough quality by any standard, leaving her little to complain about anyway. Now that dinner had been enjoyed (if impatiently rushed along by Desmond), everyone was ready for a cocktail, finding the switch to Prohibition territory less than charming.

"What I wouldn't give for a Gin Rickey," Frederick had lamented throughout the meal, loudly enough to have visibly irritated the waiter. Rosemary only hoped the lad hadn't resorted to some infantile form of retribution and sullied their food. She knew such things sometimes happened in restaurants, though not usually at those of Barbetta's caliber.

Desmond reassured him. "I've got the solution for that, old friend, a simply smashing one, just as soon as everyone has finished eating." His tone had implied they were all dawdling, which of course, had only resulted in actual dawdling given his friends' contrary tendencies. By the time they arrived in front of the alleyway where Desmond had assured them the city's very best speakeasy was located, he vibrated with excitement.

"See, here we are," he said, pointing to a half-illuminated neon sign that, after squinting, Rosemary deduced was meant to read *Red Door Antiquities & More*.

Even if she hadn't been privy to Desmond's recounting of the first time he'd happened upon the sign, she would have realized that the unlit portions weren't at all random. Only the t-i-q-u (minus the t's cross) and the o-r were lit so that it read *liquor* if one looked at it properly. Rosemary had to admit it was an ingenious way of disguising while also advertising an establishment serving illegal booze.

Illegal booze, indeed! She silently thanked whoever had ensured the continued sale of alcohol back home. Having heard tales of the stuff served in American speakeasies—drinks strong enough to render a seasoned sailor positively blotto—Rosemary wasn't quite as thrilled as Desmond to experience such atrocities for herself. A nice flowery gin or a smooth brandy was more her speed.

Desmond forged ahead and then took a sharp right, disappearing behind a thick swath of vines. When Rosemary, Vera, and Frederick caught up, they realized he'd ducked into an entrance vestibule hidden behind the foliage. Inside, he ignored a set of double doors emblazoned with the shop's name and instead turned to face a blank wall to the left. While his friends looked on with bated breath, Desmond's fingers searched the trim capping off the wainscoting until he found what he was looking for.

"Here it is," he said excitedly, gesturing for everyone to look closer. A knot in the wood featured a tiny carving of a door. "Isn't it clever? Right in plain sight, but you'd never know it, would you?"

"Positively genius!" Frederick exclaimed, his eyes sparkling.

When Desmond pressed the knot, the wall popped open to reveal a narrow corridor and a steep set of wooden stairs. Even Vera appeared amused, commenting, "The lengths I'll go for a G&T," shaking her head as she climbed.

The banister pulsed rhythmically beneath Rosemary's fingers, and her ears strained to find the source of the vibration. At the top of the stairs, Desmond knocked on a wildly crooked door that featured a miniature version of itself set at face height. When the smaller one whipped open and a pair of eyes appraised the foursome, even Desmond was taken aback. The noise of the party wafted through, finally reconciling with the thrumming of the bass and coalescing into a zippy jazz tune.

"What's the password?" the man demanded. He was barely more than a boy, Rosemary realized after catching a glimpse of the rest of his face.

"Oh, uh," Desmond stuttered. "I'm a friend of Imogene's."

The young man snorted and said, "Like I ain't heard that one a thousand times." He made to slam the door, but Desmond interrupted.

"You're Zeke, aren't you?" he asked, and when it didn't appear as though this knowledge was any more convincing than the mention of Imogene, Desmond added, "You're the one who was framed for Tillie's murder." Evidently, that wasn't quite as common knowledge as the young man's name because he hesitated. "Tell her Desmond and his British friends are here. We're expected."

Rosemary thought perhaps Desmond had overplayed his hand when the small door slammed shut with a resounding clang, but a moment later, the big one swung open, and they were all allowed inside. Zeke made a show of thoroughly checking the stairwell before closing the door behind them.

It didn't take more than a cursory glance before

Rosemary realized what Desmond had found so appealing during his previous visit—and why he had been so eager to return. He was one of the good ones, but he was still a man, and the doe-eyed cigarette girls clad in scandalously short skirts would have been enough to hold his interest.

Rosemary, however, was a tad more discerning. She noted the U-shaped cherrywood bar, finding the use of teacups instead of glasses rather charming if somewhat impractical, and appreciated the amount of work that had gone into treating all the mismatched tables and chairs with thick, shining black paint. To her chagrin, Imogene had excellent taste in decor, if not in men, and the collection of oddities lining the walls were a case in point.

She didn't have much time to linger over them because when the music stopped, the lights dimmed, and the barkeep—a woman with an arm entirely covered in tattoo ink—hiked up her skirt and climbed up on top of the bar. Conversation petered out, and the room grew marginally quieter as she began to speak.

"As you all well know," the barkeep intoned theatrically, "this place—the Red Door—exists outside the cruel confines of the law!" The drums banged, and the crowd roared.

"It's here because we refuse to submit to our oppressors—to the Volsteadian ideals that have been forced down our throats when what we want is to sate them with wine and French 75s!" Another hurrah rent

11

the air.

"But, ladies and gentlemen, tonight—" a long, dramatic pause, "tonight, we have an interloper in our midst!" The drums beat in time with Rosemary's heart, and the room seemed to pulse.

"A teetotaler—a flat tire—an utter fire extinguisher! There—"

From somewhere behind the bar, a light beamed into the crowd, searching for a moment before coming to land on Desmond. Rosemary stared, amused, as a woman stepped out of the crowd to face her friend. For a long moment, Desmond appeared utterly flabbergasted, and then a slow smile spread across his face.

The woman wore knee-high boots and a flippy skirt that turned to fringe at mid-thigh. Crimson lips complemented a halo of strawberry-blond hair styled into a wild tangle of curls. Freckles danced across a dainty nose to contrast sharply with dark, steely eyes bordered by faint laugh lines.

She reached into her bootleg, pulled out a pistol, and waved it around, "You know what we do with wet blankets around here, don't you?" she demanded. "What do we do with them, folks?"

"We light 'em up!" the crowd answered in a roar.

The woman cocked the pistol. "If you say so," she said and, with a shrug, squeezed the trigger.

Chapter Two

Rosemary's breath caught in her throat, and her eyes widened to saucers, but all that happened was that a stream of water—or perhaps something a little stronger, she couldn't be certain—spewed from the end of the pistol and hit Desmond square in the chest. He looked down at the stain, then back at the woman who'd shot him, and let out a roar of laughter.

The rest of the room followed suit. After a moment, the band resumed playing, and everyone returned to their previous conversations as if nothing out of the ordinary had occurred—and perhaps it hadn't, Rosemary realized. She also decided she felt rather silly and pasted on an amused smile to cover the gaffe.

Desmond took two steps forward and asked archly, "So this is how you treat guests, is it, Genie?"

"Only the ones I like," Imogene replied with a grin that deepened the lines near her eyes. "I'm terribly sorry to have frightened your friends," she continued, turning curiously towards the group and settling her gaze upon Rosemary. "I simply couldn't resist, you know, and of course, a few theatrics always get the drinks flowing." She gestured towards the guests, all swilling happily away.

"It's better than the last time when you pulled a real pistol on me," Desmond replied affectionately as if being held at gunpoint by a woman was every man's dream. Rosemary supposed she wouldn't have been surprised to discover some truth to the notion, especially if the woman looked like Imogene. "Meet my friends: Rosemary, Vera, and, of course, Freddie."

"I didn't really think you were going to shoot him," Rosemary blurted in self-defense. She hadn't been frightened; she wasn't a delicate, fragile lady, and it irked her to be regarded as one. That Imogene hadn't actually said anything of the sort didn't figure in Rosemary's thought process.

Imogene blinked but recovered quickly and said, "Of course, you didn't," smiling with a genuine warmth that under different circumstances would have gone some way towards softening Rosemary. Instead, she fought the instinct tooth and nail.

"Des here has told me all about you," Imogene continued, "and I wouldn't have expected to catch you by surprise." She extended a hand, which Rosemary took, still skeptical, then repeated the gesture with

14

Frederick and Vera. "He described you all in such vivid detail I feel as though we've already met."

"Likewise, of course," Vera said, "although he didn't mention that you have a predilection for the theater."

Imogene threw back her head and laughed, a throaty sound that seemed to come from deep in her belly. "I'm afraid I was rather—as you lot might say—stodgy last time he was here, and even had I been myself, I hardly think he would have compared our little vaudevillian skits to the type of professional acting you're used to." She laid a hand on Vera's arm in a friendly gesture. "Our patrons do seem to enjoy a little bit of fun, however. Might we convince you to join us one evening while you're here?" As she talked, Imogene led the group to the bar and a handful of empty stools. "What's your poison? Gin, whiskey, rum, bourbon?"

"No, no," the tattooed barkeep interrupted. When she waved an arm, Rosemary couldn't help but stare in wonder. "You'll all be wanting to try my new concoction," she continued, either oblivious to or politely ignoring Rosemary's gaze. "It's less flashy than a Blue Blazer, but it's safer, and I think it has a more complex flavor. Now I need some unbiased opinions—and a name for this drink—and since you're the guests of honor tonight, you'll be my test subjects."

Desmond bowed in the direction of the bar. "Your wish is our command."

"It ought to be," the barkeep fired back, "given that during your last visit, you accused me of murder!"

"This is Tuesday if you haven't already guessed," Desmond explained. "And I'm terribly sorry, Tuesday, as I believe I made clear during my lengthy apology. Of course, I should never have believed you capable of such an atrocity," he said solemnly.

"You're forgiven, I suppose, and either way, that's enough prostrating. Now, watch." Tuesday pulled a stack of teacups from beneath the bar and lined them up in front of Desmond and his friends. "A rinse of absinthe," she explained, pouring a nip of liquid into each cup and swirling it around. "Some sugar and an orange peel." Once those were added, she grabbed a silver cocktail shaker, spun it around in her palm, and deftly removed the lid. In went several shots of gin and a handful of ice.

Tuesday arched a brow, pulled a long match from beneath the bar, struck it, and then dipped it into each cup. Blue flames flared, and the scent of caramelized sugar, orange, and licorice rent the air for a moment before she doused each cup with a stream of chilled gin. Desmond and Frederick both let out raucous cheers, the ladies' exclamations more demure, but only just.

It went on like that throughout the evening, Tuesday mixing cocktails to the beat of the music until her hands seemed to blur. Full teacups went out, and empty ones returned to be dunked into a basin of dingy water. Rosemary chose to believe the moonshine effectively killed any germs that might have collected and sipped away on her half-clean teacup with an odd sense of pleasure. Frederick might have been forgiven—excused on account of the notion that boys would be boys, but their mother would have had an absolute conniption if she'd seen what Rosemary was doing, and the thought brought an impish smile to her face.

Desmond drained the second cup of Tuesday's new cocktail, slapping his teacup down in front of him. "Barkeep, I'll have another. What are we calling these?"

Tuesday shrugged. "I haven't decided yet."

"Well, I think you should call it the Bitter Betty," Desmond offered.

Vera shook her head. "Candied Orange Swizzle sounds better to me."

The suggestions came thick and fast then. Blue Light Special, Devil's Tonic, Flaming Sapphire, Killer Cocktail, Sweet Wicked Angel.

Rosemary's suggestion was Midnight Madness.

"Hey, how about you quit your tittering and get us some drinks," came a voice from one end of the bar. The suggestion was followed by a string of curse words that would have made a sailor blush.

Imogene rolled her eyes, took a couple of steps in the customer's direction, and leaned over the bar. "Do you

17

kiss your mother with that mouth?"

"Ain't none 'a your business who I'm kissin', 'less you wanna take a number, sweetheart."

One eyebrow arched towards her hairline as Imogene retorted, "There's not enough money in the world, buddy, but do you fellas know what my business is? This establishment, where you're no longer welcome." Her voice hardened to granite, and she flipped a switch beneath the bar. A light near the door flashed, catching Zeke's attention. "Eighty-six these boobs," she shouted.

Zeke practically flew to the bar and growled, "You heard the lady," ushering the unruly customer to his feet. "Now, scram."

Full of bluster, the man huffed out a threat. "You're giving us the bum's rush? We could have you raided, you know." His two companions glanced around, embarrassed, and shook their heads as if to indicate they would prefer not to be lumped in with their friend.

"Go. Now," Zeke said, his tone suggesting the matter was closed, and ushered the lot of them out through the rear exit.

"Sorry about that," Imogene said when they were gone, her tone belying the words, "but if you give them an inch, they'll take a mile. This place is supposed to be a haven—not an entirely safe one, certainly, but a haven just the same—and we refuse to tolerate any nonsense—no exceptions."

"You won't hear anyone at the Red Door insist the customer is always right, that's for sure," Tuesday added, "a fact those of us who work here all appreciate."

Imogene shrugged, "Nobody can be right all the time. If they want better service, they can throw a rock and find another juice joint. I hear there's one on every block in this city now, so it shouldn't prove too daunting a task."

"Too bad they'll miss out on Midnight Madness if they do." Tuesday pulled out the absinthe. "Anyone up for another round?"

Chapter Three

Imogene returned to her work, Desmond's star-filled eyes following her every move, checking in on her guests from time to time as the night wore on. Finally, when the crowd had thinned, and only a handful of patrons remained, she took off her apron, smoothed her hair, and sat next to Desmond.

Seated at his other side, Rosemary found herself caught between two conversations. To her left, Vera told Tuesday all about how her mother, a once well-known stage actress, had called in an ancient favor and arranged a meeting for Vera with a famous film producer.

"It's to discuss a role in a film that's being touted as the next big hit. It could change the trajectory of my career," Vera explained. "Or it could be an absolute flop, but I prefer to remain positive. My mother said it's practically a given, and that all I'll need to do is charm Mr. Allen."

"If that's all you've got to do, then it's settled,"

Frederick said, but Tuesday didn't look so sure. At the mention of the producer's name, she'd started, and it hadn't escaped Vera's notice.

"What is it?"

"Oh, nothing," Tuesday said quickly. "I mean, it's only that there's a film producer called Isaac Allen who comes into the speakeasy, and well, he isn't the type I'd necessarily call easy to charm."

Vera breathed a sigh of relief. "That would be Mr. Allen Junior I'll be meeting with his father, who my mother says is a dear."

Tuesday's expression remained skeptical, but she smiled anyway and wished Vera luck.

"He can't be worse than the lecherous director of the play I did last year. The man had six hands and it was a constant dance to keep them off me. One time he—"

It wasn't the first or even the fifth time Rosemary had heard the story, and instead she found herself listening in while Desmond and Imogene took the opportunity to catch up.

"How are you, really?" he asked, his voice full of concern.

Imogene waved away the question. "I'm fine. You know me; it takes a lot to ruffle my feathers."

"I do know you," Desmond replied, "and you're nothing if not resourceful, so, of course you aren't in dire straits." He kept his eyes trained on her face while he took a long sip of his drink. "However, I also know you'll gloss over the bad parts and paint everything in a positive light. I prefer the truth, warts and all."

With a small smile, Imogene acquiesced. "I suppose that lately things have been more difficult than usual, and I reckon my friends could punctuate any mention of me with the phrase 'and then she smiled thinly.' I've only myself to blame, unfortunately. One can't always speak one's mind, particularly when dealing with childish, arrogant men." Her voice was bitter, but she shook her head and smiled at Desmond. He could see exactly what she'd meant because it was a thin-lipped attempt. "But, it's all going to come out in the wash, don't you worry," Imogene promised.

"I'm positive it will, but my offer still stands, you know," Desmond said lightly, laying his hand over hers. Warning bells went off in Rosemary's head. Desmond could afford to bail Imogene out of any jam she found herself in. He'd recently come into a considerable amount of money, the estate of his dearly departed auntie having been left solely in his name, and since he'd little need for it in the first place, he had yet to spend a penny.

Rosemary pretended not to listen but kept her attention riveted on their conversation. She needed to see if Imogene would jump at whatever Des had offered and prove her intentions were dishonorable, but instead,

Imogene scowled and snatched her hand away from Desmond's. Her eyes flashed with fire, and Rosemary understood exactly what it was that had attracted him to her in the first place.

"As I said before, I won't take your money," Imogene said low enough so Rosemary had to strain her ears. "Ray might have left me with a mountain of debt, but it's my mountain, and I'll turn it into a molehill quicker than you could imagine."

"Wouldn't it be better to be in bed with me than with Lucas?" Desmond pressed. He'd explained enough about the dynamic at the Red Door for Rosemary to know Lucas Pritchett was a gangster who supplied the speakeasy with alcohol. A powerful, ambitious man with no scruples. Anyone who crossed him did so at their own risk.

Imogene arched a brow and said testily, "I'm not going to bed with anyone based on money. For love, perhaps, if I wasn't so jaded, and certainly for lust; even hate and, on occasion, out of sheer boredom—but never for money."

"I didn't mean it like that, and you know it," Desmond retorted disapprovingly.

"I know it, but it still had to be said." It was clear that, above all else, Imogene valued her independence. She was self-sufficient—more so than Rosemary herself was, she realized with a start.

"I can't get out from beneath Lucas's thumb; the Red Door falls in his territory. But my history with him goes back longer than most. He won't hurt me if that's what you're worried about. He's just angry because I rejected him again. I'll keep my nose clean, stay out of his way, and it'll all be copacetic. I promise."

Desmond sighed and shook his head, and Rosemary tuned them out, suddenly uncomfortable eavesdropping. There really was something going on between the pair, Rosemary couldn't deny it. Despite her preconceived notions, she found herself quite liking Imogene. The woman had spunk, that much was certain, and she'd also turned down Desmond's generous offer. It must have been more difficult than it had seemed to turn her back on an easy way out. Imogene might not want to date Desmond, but it didn't seem like she wanted to take advantage of him either.

Perhaps, as Vera had predicted, Imogene simply didn't find herself attracted to Desmond or believe him to be a good fit. He was a few years her junior, and Desmond, for all his positive traits, wasn't what one could call mature. Unfortunately for Desmond, Rosemary could see what all the fuss was about, and though Imogene had gone up in her estimation, so had her concern for Desmond's heart.

On Rosemary's other side, the conversation between Frederick, Vera, and Tuesday had devolved into a spirited debate about American baseball.

"It's possibly the most boring sport to ever exist," Tuesday argued. "And the spitting! I see enough of people's disgusting habits right here at the Red Door."

Imogene overheard Tuesday's comment and leaned across Desmond to tell Frederick, "It's a losing battle, I'm afraid. Believe me, I've tried."

"What an absolute waste," Frederick lamented, "to be so close to Yankee Stadium and never attend a game."

"A Yankees' fan, are you? Me, too."

Vera jabbed at her husband with her elbow and answered for him, "He's obsessed and has been reading up about it ever since we booked our passage to New York! I know far more about batting averages than I ever wanted to."

"What about it, Genie? Care to escort us to a Yankees' match tomorrow afternoon?" Desmond asked hopefully.

Imogene smirked. "We call them games here, and I'm afraid I've got to work tomorrow. You know, that thing some people have to do to earn money? I'll be at the Pennington mansion all day—"

Before he could answer, Vera interrupted, her eyes alight with excitement. "The Pennington mansion? You don't mean the home of Jade Pennington, do you?"

"That's right," Imogene nodded. "The late Jade Pennington—late *and* great, if you want my opinion.

She died about a month ago."

Vera perked up. "I've only read about her in the society pages and the tabloids, but she certainly had style, didn't she?"

"In spades," Imogene agreed. "Style, grace, and spunk. I was lucky enough to have known her quite well. She was a customer at the Red Door—the antiquities portion, of course. I certainly would have been shocked to find her up here, although, to be fair, it wouldn't have been the first time I was flabbergasted by the woman. We'll auction off most of her collection for charity—art, antiques, even her wardrobe."

Imogene had said the magic words, and Rosemary could almost hear Vera's heartbeat quicken. "You don't mean her couture pieces?" Vera breathed. "Even the famous Lanvin?"

Imogene nodded in confirmation. "An assortment of pieces, yes, and I've heard mention of the Lanvin, though I don't know all the details. I'm overseeing the antiquities portion of the estate, and that alone will fetch a pretty penny. She had more treasures stuffed into that house than the Metropolitan Museum of Art!"

"What about her family?" Vera wanted to know. "Didn't her estate fall to them?"

Imogene took another sip of her drink and shook her head either to clear an unpleasant thought or the sting off her tongue. "The bulk of it, of course; the money itself, but when it came to art and antiquities Jade was very particular. She gave it all to some society for the preservation of historic buildings. Everyone has been quite keen on the whole thing, but I'm sure at least someone is brimming with resentment. Perhaps that's why Mr. Pennington is having the house torn to the ground."

"Ooh, it sounds like quite a drama."

With a smirk, Imogene nodded. "Truly. You have no idea."

"Do tell," Vera urged. "There's little I enjoy more than a good gossip session."

"Well, I suppose it's an interesting story," Imogene said, abandoning her conversation with Desmond and launching into an explanation of the Pennington family history. "Jade had the money—scads of it, from both sides of her family. Money so old it was minted by Methuselah. It was something of a scandal when she married Charles Pennington. Firstly, because his family wasn't anywhere near as well off as Jade's—Mr. Pennington, the first, built the business on his own back and then bequeathed it to his son—and secondly, he was a solid decade younger than she was at the time. Supposedly, the match had been instigated by their families as a mutually beneficial business relationship."

"So they weren't in love?"

"Not as far as I could tell, but I'm not certain she

would have confided in me. I only met her a few years ago after my father passed away and I took over the shop. I helped her procure and, in theory, resell antiquities. There's always been a lot more of the former than the latter. Nonetheless, I conversed with her quite frequently and came to consider her a friend."

"The rags always made out that she was the queen of the society set."

Smiling, Imogene said, "She was. She had the money and the status to run the city, so, of course, she did. Even so, she treated her staff well and managed to avoid being deemed an intolerable snob. Unlike the rest of the family. Mr. Pennington is quite full of himself, constantly touting his successes, and pressing his 'miracle drug' on everyone who enters the mansion. He tries to come off as jolly, but beneath the facade, he's pompous and domineering."

Pausing for a moment, Imogene worried at the beaded necklace highlighting her impressive décolletage.

"Then there are the children, grown, of course," she continued the story, "but still living in the mansion. Colette is frightfully frivolous, and though I haven't spent much time with Oscar, Jade used to say he and his father were cut from the same cloth. I don't have high hopes he won't turn into an utter cad. Did I mention Mr. Pennington's new fiancée is the same age as his daughter, Colette? It must seem awkward for a father and daughter to be engaged at the same time, and Ruby's just the kind of conniving gold digger you'd expect a man his age to fall for. An utter cliché."

Vera's eyes sparkled with interest. "I'm intrigued by the family drama, but the more important question is: when is the auction?"

"Not until next week, but would you all like to come by and have a preview?"

"Yes, that sounds lovely!" Vera clapped her hands in anticipation. "There's not much in this world I enjoy more than shopping, and a chance to take a look at Jade Pennington's collection—what a coup!"

"It would also be a coup for me should you decide to purchase anything. My friend Pippa, who's organizing the event, will be ever so grateful. She's young, trying to make her way up the ranks, and needs all the help she can get."

"Glad to be of service, then. Of course we'll be there," Desmond said quickly, answering for the group. "Vera will help preserve quite a few historic buildings, mark my words." The comment earned him a glare, but Rosemary could tell her friend's heart wasn't in it. Vera didn't have stars in her eyes. She had diamanté crystals—vintage ones like the kind used for expensive couture.

Amongst the group, Frederick alone appeared less than thrilled at the prospect. "You want to spend the day inside a stuffy old mansion?" he asked, bewildered.

"You might find something you like, you know," Imogene urged him. "Some of the sculptures are quite lovely."

"Unless they're in the likeness of a scantily clad female, I'm afraid my Freddie couldn't care less," Vera said of her husband. "The man would live with bare walls if left to his own devices, so the idea of antique shopping probably sounds like an afternoon of hell to him."

Frederick grimaced and said, "She's spot-on, but she's also quite stunning, entirely out of my league, and my wife, so I suppose I don't have much choice, do I?"

"Oh, Freedie boy," Desmond said, knowing he'd already won, "we'll make it up to you."

"With box seats, you'll make it up to me," Frederick replied sullenly, only moderately placated by Vera's thousand-watt smile in his direction.

Chapter Four

Rosemary had begun to regret her choice of footwear several blocks before reaching the Pennington mansion. The nearest subway stop was further away than Desmond had thought, and though he'd promised they'd be able to acquire a lift, it seemed Rosemary's unfortunate luck with cabs was to be as persistent as it was frustrating. The blister that had begun to form shortly into the walk had ruptured at least two blocks earlier, and the heel of her shoe dug into the tender flesh with every step.

"There she is," Desmond declared when a figure up ahead raised an arm to wave in the group's direction. He put a spring in his step that Rosemary couldn't match, making her the last to greet Imogene after taking several moments to catch up.

"Good morning," Rosemary said as brightly as she could under the circumstances, her smile not quite reaching her eyes.

Imogene hesitated, her brows drawing together. "I do hope you enjoyed The Roosevelt and that the accommodations lived up to your usual standards."

"Quite comfortable," Desmond assured her quickly, but it wasn't his opinion Imogene desired.

"The Roosevelt is a lovely hotel, of course. Top-notch," Rosemary replied, grimacing slightly as her shoe sliced across her already tender heel. "It's just rather a long walk." Her gaze fell on Desmond with some accusation.

Imogene's expression cleared. "It's happened to me loads of times. I can barely feel my toes anymore. But you're in luck; I've got a swath of moleskin in my handbag that should be enough to provide some relief."

"Thank you," Rosemary replied gratefully. "You're a godsend."

"I'll show you to the nearest lavatory just as soon as we get inside. The house is just there." Imogene gestured towards a multi-level limestone masterpiece of the Victorian era. Her tone was bitter when she explained, "The family—some of them anyway—wants something more modern, so the house itself will be stripped of anything deemed fit to reuse, then demolished. Blasphemous, if you ask me."

"A crying shame," agreed Rosemary.

Imogene nodded, then shook her head as if to clear the unpleasant thought and rang the doorbell. "Hello, Mrs.

Doon," she said politely when a harassed-looking maid opened the door.

"Who's there?" the maid demanded, dispensing with the usual pleasantries and looking upon Rosemary and company suspiciously.

Although she stiffened, Imogene's voice remained even as she explained. "These are my friends from London, come for a preview of the auction. Mr. Desmond Cooper, Mrs. Rosemary Lillywhite, and Mr. and Mrs. Frederick Woolridge of Woolridge & Sons textiles. They're quite well vetted, I can assure you, and keen to see Mrs. Pennington's impressive collection."

Rosemary was impressed with Imogene's quick and thorough description, but Mrs. Doon did not appear to feel similarly, nor was she prepared to budge from her position blocking their entry. "You're supposed to use the servants' entrance around the block."

Imogene's face reddened at the comment, but before she could protest, a voice boomed from inside, "Woolridge & Sons, you say?"

Mrs. Doon sighed, opened the door wider, and stepped back to reveal a handsome middle-aged gentleman who carried himself with an air of importance. "Woolridge, Woolridge—" He snapped his fingers, "Cecil Woolridge, isn't it?"

"Cecil Woolridge is my father, sir. I'm Frederick, and I presume you're the esteemed Mr. Pennington?"

The man nodded. "In the flesh. A pleasure to meet you all. I've heard of your company, of course, even though textiles aren't my area of expertise. I'm in pharmaceuticals, you know," he said, puffing his chest, "but there's nothing wrong with textiles. We all do need our chairs covered, isn't that right? It seems there's money everywhere, just begging to be made, even in the strangest of places."

"Yes, quite," Frederick agreed, ignoring what sounded to Rosemary like a veiled insult. She wondered how many men of Mr. Pennington's type her brother and father were forced to endure for the sake of business. Frederick proved himself deft at the task when he added, "It all spends the same, doesn't it?"

Mr. Pennington's lip twitched, and he appraised Frederick with newfound respect. "Indeed, indeed. Well, what are you waiting out there for, then? Come on in, have a look around."

He ushered them into a vast entrance hall dominated by an enormous marble cantilevered staircase. Unfortunately, the ornate architecture could hardly be appreciated, suffocated as it was by the overwhelming volume of decorative detritus—art, sculpture, and bric-a-brac—crammed into the space. In preparation for the auction, many of the items had had labels affixed to them, which only added to the clutter.

An enormous oil-on-canvas portrait of a handsome,

impeccably dressed Jade Pennington dominated the central wall above the stairs facing the front entrance, the rest of the family represented in the many other pieces hanging frame-to-frame around it. His throat thick, Mr. Pennington explained, "My late wife had excellent—if not excessive—taste. She was practically a saint in every other way, so I indulged her."

Rosemary immediately sympathized and softened towards the man. "I'm very sorry for your loss," she said with sincerity. It had been nearly two years since Rosemary had lost her husband, and despite her efforts to move on, every so often, the grief came rushing back to feel as fresh as ever.

Something akin to pain flitted across Mr. Pennington's face, but his mood remained buoyant. "That's very kind," he replied, his eyes not quite meeting Rosemary's and landing on Mrs. Doon instead. "Eleanor, please do stop scowling at our guests. We don't want them returning to London thinking Americans possess no manners, do we?"

Mrs. Doon didn't appear to care about Rosemary and her friends' opinions regarding Americans, but she nodded and smiled—albeit blankly—at her employer's statement all the same. "Yes, Mr. Pennington. It's none of my nevermind, of course, who you want to allow in through the front door." Blatantly ignoring Imogene's narrow-eyed glance, she made her excuses and then stalked away into the bowels of the house.

"Don't mind Mrs. Doon, the old fossil," said Mr. Pennington. "She's a pill, but she knows the household in and out. Do any of you fancy a drink?" He glanced back at his guests and winked. "We had our cellar filled to the brim before the dark days began, so it's all perfectly legal, of course. No law against actually *drinking* alcohol. Quite the circular problem, eh?"

It seemed Mr. Pennington had already begun to enjoy the fruits of his foresight despite the early hour of the day. In his wake trailed the scent of whiskey mingled with cigar smoke and, if Rosemary wasn't mistaken, sandalwood. She wondered how much gin one might have to stockpile in order to be soused before noon on the regular.

Desmond hung back, veritably clinging to Imogene's side, hardly noticing his surroundings. The mansion—calling it a house would have been a gross understatement—looked as if it could rate a feature in *Architectural Digest*. Mr. Pennington took a meandering route through the front of the house, which consisted of a drawing room, salon, smoking room, and finally, a morning room with a lovely view of Park Avenue. Rosemary's townhouse, though quite spacious, wasn't nearly as grandiose and could have fit easily into the entrance hall with room to spare! Whatever the rear of the place consisted of was a mystery she hoped to have the chance to uncover.

When Rosemary winced with pain, Mr. Pennington hastened to ask, "Are you feeling quite all right? You look a little green around the gills. If it's indigestion, I've got just the thing—Bella-quil." He winked and said, "for a tranquil belly. You'll find some in the lavatory, of course." He pointed down a corridor to the left and then turned his attention to an explanation about the sconces.

When his back was turned, Imogene caught Rosemary's eye and then Vera's. She smiled wryly, her eyes flicking towards Mr. Pennington with amusement. For a moment, Rosemary felt as though she were back in school, joking with her friends behind the headmistress's back. The feeling only strengthened when she recognized the set of Vera's jaw and knew her friend had been forced to chew the inside of her lip to keep from laughing.

"It's this way." Imogene guided Rosemary away from the rest of the group and through a door much plainer than the rest. Inside, she discovered a combination water closet and bathing room with a white porcelain bathing tub, a toilet, and two sinks.

"This is some loo," Rosemary said, eliciting a smile from Imogene as she extracted the square of soft cloth from her purse and handed it over.

"It's the cat's pajamas. What I wouldn't give for a bathtub like that." A devilish gleam lit Imogene's eyes.

"Just think how much gin it would hold."

Aghast, Rosemary's eyes popped wide. She'd heard of bathtub gin but thought the tales exaggerated. When Imogene offered a cheeky wink, Rosemary schooled her expression and tried to hide her chagrin by searching through her handbag for a sticking plaster to affix the protective material to her heel. Finding none, she let out the smallest of sighs.

"You need a Band-Aid?" Imogene asked, then when Rosemary's brows beetled in confusion, she elaborated. "Adhesive bandage. I'm sure I can scare one up."

Without waiting for an answer, Imogene unabashedly opened cabinet doors until she found a small box marked with red crosses and the name Johnson & Johnson on the front.

"We call them sticking plasters." Rosemary accepted the box and went to work affixing the padding to her heel and sliding her feet back into her shoes. "That feels much better. Thank you."

"My pleasure."

During the return trip to join her friends, Rosemary took a longer look at the series of paintings and photographs lining the corridor. One image stopped her in her tracks and elicited an exclamation of appreciation.

"Spectacular, isn't it?" Imogene pointed to the dress. "That's by Paul Poiret. He's a French designer."

"Yes. I know." Rosemary hadn't been looking at the

dress so much as the brush strokes the artist had used to convey its texture. "It's lovely."

The flame-colored underskirt featured a delicately beaded hemline that reminded Rosemary of *langues de chat* biscuits, so named because of their resemblance to a cat's tongue. The pattern repeated in four more beaded layers, the longest nearly transparent but for the beading, becoming more solid as they rose to end in gold silk at the sleeveless top with more beading at the neckline. Vera would kill for that dress, Rosemary thought. Or if not kill, at least maim.

"This must have been painted fairly recently, given the style of the dress." Not that Jade hadn't worn something equally stylish in each photograph or painting. Looking closer, Rosemary remarked, "And did the woman never age? She had exquisite skin." So pale and with a youthful blush.

"Pond's cold cream. Jade swore by it. Went through buckets of the stuff and was particular about taking any sun."

Reluctantly, because she would have liked to peruse the artwork longer, Rosemary accompanied Imogene back to meet up with her friends.

More curious over the mention of a collection of baseball memorabilia located in the smoking room, Frederick seemed reluctant to join them as the others followed Mr. Pennington into the drawing room. He chattered all the way, mostly regarding his pharmaceutical company.

"We've got a pill for everything, or we will have in short order. The advances we've made with atropine alone are revolutionizing the industry; at varying levels, it's an effective treatment for at least half a dozen different ailments. Our research is backed by top scientists, of course, using the latest methods, so it's all perfectly safe," he boasted.

Even Rosemary couldn't argue that such an accomplishment warranted a certain level of satisfaction.

"We've been working on a decoction to help women through the birthing process, but it's in the early stages. Too late for some." Mr. Pennington's gaze flicked briefly to a photo of Jade, heavy with child and wearing a stylish maternity dress.

"A worthwhile endeavor, indeed," Vera said. "You should be quite proud, Mr. Pennington."

The statement hung there for a fraction of a second before the tinkling sound of a woman's laugh cut through the air. "Of one thing you can be sure is that Daddy is always *quite proud* of all his accomplishments."

Vera bristled at the comment, but ever the consummate actress, the only clue was an infinitesimal straightening of her spine that only Rosemary noticed.

It took a moment to locate the source of the comment,

so stuffed with furniture was the spacious drawing room—settees, tables, lamps, armchairs covered in chintz, an odd footstool set here and there. It looked like a church jumble sale, except every item bore a patina of ostentation. When Mr. Pennington described his late wife's taste as excessive, he hadn't been exaggerating.

Across one chaise longue was draped a young woman so pale and lithe as to conjure to Rosemary's mind an image of Le Fanu's lady vampire, Carmilla. She wore a form-fitting black velvet dress with a plunging neckline, though why she would have been dressed so formally at noon on a Tuesday was anyone's guess—perhaps for the same reason they'd found her father half-spifflicated. She held a short silver cigarette holder in one hand, which she used to gesture with more than actually smoked.

"Coco, please, put a lid on it," Mr. Pennington intoned with a shake of his head. "We have guests, don't we?"

The woman blew out a ring of smoke, extinguished the cigarette in a nearby crystal ashtray, and then unfolded herself from her seat to make introductions. "Colette Pennington," she said in a tone that suggested stating her name was more effort than she would truly care to make, peering disinterestedly at the newcomers from beneath a fringe of jet-black hair. "And that's my younger brother, Oscar, if you didn't know."

Colette waved in the general direction of a man who

nobody, not even the usually observant Rosemary, had noticed and then sunk back onto the chaise and relit her cigarette.

"My son," Mr. Pennington boomed proudly, "and my right-hand man—the future of Pennington Pharmaceuticals." He might have been announcing the King's presence, for all the pomp and circumstance, and Oscar's face bloomed into a blush his father didn't seem to notice. The younger man wasn't entirely unattractive, bearing a marked resemblance to his father, but it was as if the reconfiguration of features had somehow been scrambled. His nose, for instance, was a carbon copy of the elder Mr. Pennington's but was positioned closer to his eyes in a way that vaguely reminded Rosemary of a cubist painting.

"Good afternoon and welcome," Oscar said politely after another round of introductions. "To what do we owe the pleasure?" His eyes had flicked momentarily to Imogene, who, Rosemary guessed, wasn't typically privy to afternoon drinks in the drawing room, but there was no ill will in his question as far as she could tell—only curiosity.

"Miss Quinn has brought along some rather interesting friends," Mr. Pennington explained. "They've come all the way from London for business, though I would think such company," his eyebrows jiggled flirtatiously in the ladies' direction, "ought to be counted under the pleasure column, am I right, lads?"

Neither Frederick nor Desmond could deny him the point, so they both nodded while Colette Pennington smirked. The expression on her face softened somewhat when her father began to pour the drinks and further when Mrs. Doon ushered in another young man. "Mr. Scott for Miss Colette," Mrs. Doon said, her tone disapproving. Rosemary wondered if there was anyone she actually approved of.

"Finn, darling, where have you been?" Colette demanded with a pout.

The young man smiled indulgently in her direction and swiftly strode the length of the room, depositing a peck on her upturned cheek. "Oscar," he said, smiling in a friendly manner before approaching the man of the house and offering his greetings.

A second round of introductions was made, and during their course, Rosemary noticed Imogene appeared impatient or perhaps out of place. The latter theory proved correct when Finn—Phineas Clark, of the Pennsylvania Clarks, betrothed to the imperious Coco—regarded Imogene curiously.

"Miss Quinn, isn't that right?" he asked politely. "You're the art expert, yes?"

"Not quite," Imogene replied smoothly. "Antiquities are my forte. And what is it that you do?"

For a moment, the young Finn appeared caught off

guard, but his face quickly smoothed back into a neutral expression. He opened his mouth to answer, but Colette beat him to it. "Finn's family owns a famous paper company, of course," she said, as though anyone who didn't already know must be quite daft indeed.

"Toilet tissue, isn't it?" Imogene asked innocently, a smile playing around her lips and nearly teasing one from Rosemary as well. She had to give Desmond's American friend her due: Imogene certainly had guts and, much like Frederick, no qualms about delivering underhanded insults to those who considered themselves her betters.

Even Mr. Pennington appeared amused, but Finn's feathers remained unruffled. If Rosemary wasn't quite mistaken, he was a man who didn't lack confidence. Or, perhaps, he'd wound up a cheeky retort but was robbed of the chance to deliver it, for just then, the party was joined by a woman who made Coco Pennington look positively plain by comparison.

"Where's my sweetie pie?"

CHAPTER FIVE

Rosemary spun around to locate the source of the voice, and for a moment, she thought perhaps she'd taken a wrong turn and ended up in front of a Broadway stage. Framed in the doorway stood a woman in a getup so extravagant it simply had to be a costume.

Diamonds dripped from her ears, throat, and wrists, and she wore a slinky dress that landed just above a pair of exquisite patent-leather pumps. A long slit running up to her mid-thigh, however, contradicted the appropriate length of the skirt thoroughly enough to capture the attention of every eye in the room. Frederick's, for instance, nearly popped out of his head, but his proximity to his wife kept them mostly focused on the floor.

"Ruby, darling," Mr. Pennington said, his voice significantly softer than it had been thus far. "There you are." It was obvious from how his tongue rolled over her name that Mr. Pennington was positively smitten with the new arrival. "I thought we'd lost you, my love."

At the endearment, Colette's face drained of color and hardened into granite. "We should be so lucky," she said under her breath. Both Ruby and Mr. Pennington ignored the comment, the latter with considerably more effort than the former.

Ruby's eyes flicked between each of the people assembled in the drawing room, lingering slightly longer over Frederick and Desmond, validating Imogene's description of her as the type to use her feminine wiles as a means of manipulation. She sauntered towards Mr. Pennington, hips swiveling seductively, and draped herself over his shoulder.

"You should have told me we were expecting company," she purred in a soft, breathy voice, not unlike a child's and yet still sultry. "I would have dolled myself up." A wet-sounding kiss landed square on Mr. Pennington's lips and lingered there long enough to send a wave of discomfort through the room.

"Oh, darling, you look sensational, of course," Mr. Pennington replied when Ruby finally pulled away, his eyes sparkling. Rosemary couldn't help but watch his daughter's reaction, and the expression on Colette's face did not disappoint. At first, she looked as though she might be sick and then like she was contemplating ripping Ruby's hair out by the fistful.

Beside her, Finn followed Frederick's lead and kept his eyes trained on the floor, but Rosemary thought she detected a measure of amusement at his future in-laws' display of affection. When Colette's gaze flicked to him, he quickly schooled his features into a neutral expression and leaned closer to sling his arm around her shoulders.

Rosemary took a long slug of her drink, less for fortitude and more to cover the amused grin she couldn't fully suppress, and then yet another round of introductions ensued. Though it would have been quite impossible to forget anyone's name by now, Rosemary highly doubted Ruby Snow had been paying attention. Furthermore, the woman didn't appear bothered by the palpable tension rolling off Colette—or, perhaps, she was so utterly self-involved she hadn't noticed.

And yet how could one blame Colette for feeling bitter? Rosemary wondered. The women were close enough in age that Ruby could have been her sister. Age wasn't the only similarity between the two. Both women gave off vanity like a cloud of cigarette smoke, sharing the opinion that more was more when it came to fashion. Where commonality could have brought the two closer, Rosemary got the impression it created rivalry instead. Nobody in their right mind would assume these women enjoyed a stepmother-stepdaughter relationship. Or any relationship at all.

"Mr. Pennington." A male voice cut through the tension. In the doorway, a man in a sharp servant's uniform stood at attention next to a young woman. "Miss Langley is here to see you. She says she's expected."

"Ah yes, Leo. She is expected. Come in, Miss Langley," said Mr. Pennington, who introduced Leo Sterling as his man-of-all-work.

Tight-lipped and proper, Leo reminded Rosemary of her steadfast and protective butler, Wadsworth. What would he be doing right now? Doing the math to calculate the time difference, she realized he'd be sound asleep. Probably with Dash curled up on the rug next to his bed. Travel was fine and a wonderful way to learn about different cultures, but home carried its own appeal.

"Thank you, Leo." Ruby stressed her use of the man's given name. "Mr. Pennington isn't in need of any further assistance," Ruby commanded, a sharper edge to her voice than she'd used thus far. "That will be all." Her lip turned up ever so slightly at one corner into a self-satisfied sneer that left the impression she quite enjoyed lording her authority over the staff.

To his credit, Leo refused to rise to the unspoken challenge and, in fact, looked right through Ruby as though she wasn't there at all. Having been dismissed, he merely nodded and practically faded from view, leaving Miss Langley standing alone.

She wore a smart but modest skirt and jacket, and although her silhouette was slightly less captivating than Ruby's, it was still slim enough to be considered fashionable. Hair cropped into a sensible bob curled around a pretty face—again, not as striking as Ruby's, but Oscar Pennington didn't seem to find it lacking in charm. He perked up noticeably as she entered and could hardly tear his eyes away.

"I'm terribly sorry, sir," she apologized, looking to Imogene for commiseration. "I wasn't aware the room was occupied, only that Miss Quinn could be found here. We'd planned to catalog the drawing room today, but, of course, we can rearrange our schedule if it pleases." Her tone cast a veneer of politeness over the underlying tension shown in her stiff posture and the pinching around her mouth.

"Miss Langley works for the auction house," Imogene explained, attempting to shift the focus off the annoyed woman. "She's coordinating the event—no small feat given the scope of Jade—Mrs. Pennington's collection."

Rosemary dredged the name Pippa from her memory of the previous evening, guessing Miss Langley to be the ambitious friend Imogene had described. "Now, if you'll excuse us, we must get on with our work. Shall I give my guests a proper tour and allow you to continue your day?" This she directed towards Mr. Pennington, who either didn't notice or chose to ignore her pointed tone.

With a wave of his hand, he dismissed Imogene, stating, "You go on ahead, Miss Quinn. I'm genuinely intrigued by our British guests, and surely I'm qualified to conduct a tour of my own home. I promise to point out the important pieces."

Imogene's jaw clenched, and she looked something like Colette had moments before—as though she might spit fire—but put in the effort to remain calm. "Well then, I suppose I'll catch up with my friends when you're through," Imogene said and stalked towards the rear of the drawing room, Pippa in tow.

Oscar, who up until now had remained firmly planted in his seat, squirmed uncomfortably, and the motion caught Finn's attention. He took the hint and raised his hand. "Not so fast, please. I believe Oscar here wished to bend Miss Langley's ear." When Oscar still didn't speak, Finn added pointedly, "I believe he had a question about one of the paintings," and waved a hand vaguely at the cluttered wall full of art.

"Of course. I'd be happy to answer your questions, Mr. Pennington," said Miss Langley, gathering herself to her full height and peering at Oscar expectantly.

"Please, Miss Langley, call me Oscar. Such formality is hardly necessary," he replied, finally finding his voice. It was smooth and steady when he said, "It's the one there, in the center, that I've always fancied."

Oscar peered at the painting for a long moment, lost in a memory. "I thought perhaps you could tell me a little bit more about it. I might even consider hanging onto that one. After all, we wouldn't want to get rid of every one of Mother's treasures, now would we?" There was a softness to his tone, a sensitivity that he, alone of the Pennington family, seemed to possess.

Miss Langley shook her head, but from across the room, Ruby muttered under her breath, "Depends on who you mean by we."

"He means our family." Colette cast Ruby a defiant glare that said she didn't count her father's fiancée as part of that group.

"Coco, we have company," Mr. Pennington warned in a light voice that carried an undercurrent of seriousness—one Colette blatantly ignored.

"*You* have company, Father," she said in the tone of a bored teenager. "The rest of us simply live here."

"I'm afraid I'm not certain," Miss Langley said loudly, looking pointedly at Oscar and attempting to defuse the tension, "about the history of that painting. I could ask our art appraiser to come in tomorrow, unless Miss Quinn knows its origin. My apologies, sir." Her eyes flicked towards the door as though she'd like to make an escape, though Rosemary couldn't tell whether the desire was due to Oscar's attention or the tension radiating off Colette.

Imogene peered at the painting for a long moment and shook her head. "I'm sorry, I won't be much help, either," she said, abashed. "As I said, my expertise lies with antiquities."

Before the discussion, Rosemary had already noticed the canvas and found herself impressed with Jade Pennington's—and now her son's—taste. "If I'm not mistaken, that is a still life by impressionist Mary Cassatt. I've seen her work before. The brush strokes are unmistakably fluent and angular, reflecting the composition's slashing diagonals," she blurted, surprising even herself.

As if drawn to do so, Rosemary moved closer and pointed to the corner of the painting where she could just make out a set of initials. "She normally signed her full name, but occasionally, only her initials. I would hang on to it, particularly if it has sentimental value. It will fetch a pretty penny now, but if you have patience, I suspect you'll find it worth quite a lot more in a few years."

Everyone in the room, save her friends, who already knew of Rosemary's prowess, stared. "I studied art and art history at university," she said by way of explanation, suddenly regretting having stepped on Pippa Langley's toes as Imogene's mouth set into an even thinner line than it had been before.

"How very fortunate for us," exclaimed Mr.

Pennington. "It looks as though Mrs. Lillywhite here has saved the auction house some time. Perhaps there are other pieces she might have luck identifying—not that we'd ask her to sing for her supper, of course." He laughed, a great booming that echoed off the cluttered walls to vibrate loudly in Rosemary's ear.

"I'd be delighted," she said, lacking any other polite response.

Mr. Pennington smiled and clapped his hands. "Shall we resume our tour? Perhaps Miss Langley and Miss Quinn should join us. They might even learn a thing or two about art."

The unflattering aspersion cast by Mr. Pennington's comment sent the temperature of Imogene's gaze plummeting a few more degrees and even teased an irritated nose flare from Oscar.

CHAPTER SIX

Obliged to fall in with Mr. Pennington's wishes, Imogene and Pippa tagged along behind the others even though they both had a pile of work to complete. Despite his annoyance, Oscar seemed content to follow after Pippa much as Desmond did after Imogene, leaving Rosemary, Frederick, and Vera to bear the conversational brunt of Mr. Pennington's attention. Well, aside from Ruby, who attached herself to his arm like a leech.

While he pointed out those items he felt would interest his guests, Ruby let a series of sighs and breathy comments indicate her opinions, which were not favorable. Ruby, it seemed, preferred a sleek, modern design with plenty of sparkle and shine. Everything else she deemed too stuffy or boring.

"Aren't you just the little magpie." Colette offered her future-stepmother a daggered look. "What's the saying? All that glitters is not gold." By the look on her face,

Rosemary thought Colette would have liked to have added the word *digger* to the end of the quote. It seemed Colette had only joined the tour to poke at Ruby.

Rosemary watched the exchange, saw Colette become more irritated by the second, and concluded that Imogene had been as spot-on in her description of the Pennington clan as she had the house itself.

As predicted, Rosemary had never seen anything quite like the mansion. Every piece of furniture was polished to a shine, not a speck of dust to be found, and none of the mirrors were smudged with fingerprints (the horror!). It seemed Mrs. Doon, the old dinosaur of a maid, ran a tight ship.

"It's like a museum," Vera said in awe when Mr. Pennington casually referred to a reticulated Chinese vase with intricate gilt filigree and a graceful curve.

"If you mean loaded with dusty artifacts from the past," Ruby muttered just loud enough to bring a scowl to Colette's face. Mr. Pennington shot her a quelling look, which she ignored. "I prefer to look to the future."

"If we turn our backs on the past, we will never learn from it." Rosemary hadn't meant to chide, or even to speak at all, but couldn't seem to help herself. "And I haven't noticed so much as a speck of dust on anything in this house. Your staff is very dedicated."

Mr. Pennington preened at the compliment, but Ruby sniffed with derision. "Your standards must be quite low. I've found them quite lacking."

"Maybe if you hadn't alienated the maids, they'd be more considerate," Colette pointed out with a false sense of helpfulness that left Ruby with nothing more to say.

By the time the tour ascended to the third floor, Rosemary had become fatigued by both the immensity of Jade Pennington's collection and the sound of her husband's voice. He was, as Imogene described, pompous and overbearing beneath his cheerful exterior.

At the top of the staircase, Mr. Pennington marched across a great expanse of parquet floor and approached a set of grand double doors. "This level consists of the library and," he pointed to corridors on either side, "the family bedrooms and guest suites."

Reluctantly, Rosemary followed the rest of the group into the library. "It's my favorite room in the house," Mr. Pennington announced bombastically, leading them into a cavernous room. "I'll hate to see it go."

"There, there, my sweetie," Ruby cooed. "No turning back now. You agreed we needed something more modern. We've talked about this. We'll build you a new library. A better one."

Mr. Pennington allowed himself to be convinced, but looking around, Rosemary could see why it was his favorite room. Leather-bound books lined the floor-to-ceiling shelves except on the east-facing side. There, a set of windows framed a terrace garden filled with elaborate topiaries and potted roses. Rosemary longed to curl up in one of the overstuffed armchairs and sink into a good book almost as much as she yearned to take a spin on one of the rolling ladders that granted access to the upper bookshelves. It took a concerted effort to tamp down both urges.

In the center of the library, illuminated by a shaft of light coming in through the windows, rested an enormous rug bearing the Pennington family crest. Rosemary recognized it from the shield on one of the suits of armor lining one of the second-floor corridors. Or had it been the first floor? She could hardly keep track and sincerely hoped Mr. Pennington intended to refrain from another long and, thanks to the many whiskeys he'd enjoyed, rather rambling explanation of why royal blue had been chosen in place of navy. As it was, she feared the first had been permanently seared into her memory.

The desire to settle in this room might have had something to do with it being the only one she'd seen so far that wasn't crammed to the brim with art and knick-knacks. As such, Rosemary found it an oasis of peace. Comfortable chairs, a sofa, and a pair of occasional tables grouped in front of a fireplace that jutted into the room made a perfect spot for quiet conversation.

Not that any conversation would be quiet so long as

Mr. Pennington was around. The man spoke in booming tones as if a moment's silence would kill him. Even as Rosemary admitted this unflattering opinion to herself, Mr. Pennington pointed to a pair of crossed swords hanging on the wall and began to detail their history.

"It is said," he pontificated as he took one of the swords down from the wall, "that once the steel has tasted blood, it becomes a craving. I don't know about all that, but they're well-balanced weapons and sharp as the devil."

Eyes alight with the chance to show off, Mr. Pennington handed the sword to Desmond, who accepted it with little interest, made a show of testing its weight, then passed it over to Frederick. Meanwhile, Mr. Pennington took down its mate and brandished the second sword as if fighting an imaginary adversary. Frederick did the same.

"Nice grip. Feels good in the hand, and you were right about the balance. Excellent workmanship," Frederick complimented the weapon.

"What do you say, son? Are you brave enough to clash steel with me and give the ladies a bit of a show? I promise I'm accomplished enough at swordplay to avoid bloodshed, so your young wife won't have to worry that you'll be taken away in pieces. It's only your pride I'll shred to tatters."

Whatever Frederick thought of that, he only allowed

himself the faintest twist of his lip. "I'd be delighted." So saying, he took a firmer grip on the sword and settled into his en garde stance.

"Give us some room." Mr. Pennington boomed out a laugh. "We wouldn't want to nick an innocent bystander."

Rosemary took Vera's arm as everyone stepped back to form a loose circle around the fencers, feeling a minor tremble run through her friend.

Ignoring proper fencing etiquette, Mr. Pennington swung his sword, Frederick parried then offered a riposte, and the match began. Metal sang against metal while the opponents tested each other's skills. While Mr. Pennington put plenty of power behind his attacks, Frederick had more reach and speed.

Vera needn't have feared for the safety of her husband's skin. As beads of sweat appeared on Mr. Pennington's brow, Frederick parried thrust after thrust without putting in a great deal of effort.

"It's a shame hand fans have gone out of fashion." Vera tilted her head so only Rosemary could hear. "I didn't know Freddie could move like that. It's heating me up."

While Mr. Pennington relied on brute force, Freddie moved with an elegant grace that any woman might admire. Any woman except Rosemary.

"Ew, Vera. That's my brother you're talking about."

"Those swords are worth some scratch." Imogene leaned forward for a closer look. "What do you think, Pippa?"

"With the eagle pommel," Pippa assessed. "I'd say they were made by Fredrick Wilhelm Widmann. They'd generate some interest now, but they'll be worth more later. A good investment."

Shamelessly listening in, Vera poked her sharp elbow into Rosemary's ribs. "These two are all business. There's a fine-looking man showing his prowess, and all they can think about is the provenance of the swords."

This must have tickled Imogene because she barked out a laugh. "Far be it from me to offer a bawdy comment on another woman's husband."

After a suitable time, Freddie expertly flicked his wrist, handily disarmed his opponent, and ended the match with his sword an inch from Mr. Pennington's throat. After a moment's pause, Frederick lowered the weapon.

"Well done, my boy. Well done." Where Rosemary might have expected Mr. Pennington to be a sore loser, he surprised her with a hearty laugh. "I can see this wasn't your first foray into the art of swordplay."

"Sorry, old chap. I suppose I should have said. While my sister spent her time with musty old paintings, I was on the fencing team at university," Frederick admitted with a grin, then offered some consolation. "Had you invited me to a round of billiards, you'd have come out on top. Chasing balls around the baize is Desmond's game."

From his position on the sidelines, Oscar said wryly, "And to think I wasted my time in school studying biology."

Mr. Pennington's booming laugh sounded again. "Is that so? I'll have to show you my second-favorite room in the house." He pinned Desmond with a look. "Indulge me in a round of pool, young fellow? We'll celebrate my win with a snifter of imported brandy unless you'd prefer whisky instead. All imported, of course. I only drink the very best."

"Delighted to," Desmond replied.

CHAPTER SEVEN

Frederick might have been willing to break up the long-winded house tour with a round of billiards, but neither his wife nor his sister shared his enthusiasm. The younger Penningtons, Finn included, had also grown weary with the familiar grounds of the mansion. For Pippa and Imogene, each room represented a portion of work that had yet to be completed, and as such, they were both eager to get back to it. Nevertheless, nobody was willing to speak up, so they followed Mr. Pennington back into the corridor.

As the rather large group exited the library, a rustling noise rent the air, coming from the direction of Mrs. Pennington's rooms, followed by a strangled cry and the sound of a heavy object thudding to the ground. Mr. Pennington quickened his step and took a sharp right. "That will be Mrs. Russel wrestling with Jade's wardrobe, no doubt. She probably ought not to have come out of retirement for this, but there wasn't any convincing her. She said she owed it to fashion, or some such silliness."

He had said the magic words, at least for Vera. Her eyes lit with a genuine interest for the first time since the unintentionally amusing family portrait gallery on the second floor. It seemed Mr. Pennington had devoted several years of his life to growing a fine mustache. At the height of its glory, he'd taken to waxing the thing into a ridiculous series of curlicues, some of them quite comical.

At the other end of a short corridor, a luxurious sitting room served as antechamber to Mrs. Pennington's boudoir. "Mrs. Russel!" Colette exclaimed when the group entered to find a deeply wrinkled older woman kneeling in the center of a massive wardrobe bigger than Rosemary's bedroom. "Are you all right?" Colette rushed forward to offer assistance.

A slip of a thing, Mrs. Russel's petite delicacy had given way to fragility some years earlier. She sat on the floor amid a mound of shoeboxes that, until recently, had been piled on one of the high shelves above and wore a rueful smile proving her none the worse for wear.

With a wave of her Lilliputian hand, Mrs. Russel tried to refuse Colette's ministrations but ultimately allowed herself to be transferred to a comfortable chair. "Thank you, dear," she said affectionately, proving the feeling a mutual one. "I'm right as rain, though it seems I've got myself in over my head both figuratively and literally. I don't suppose you could spare a worker bee or two to help clear these boxes and crates?" She directed the question towards Pippa in her position as auction coordinator.

Colette answered before Pippa could open her mouth. "I'll help," she offered to the surprise of nearly everyone in the room, "if you like."

"I'm happy to lend a hand as well." Vera spoke up nearly as unexpectedly. She received a grateful smile from Mrs. Russel and an odd glance from Mr. Pennington.

"Of course, we wouldn't have our guests performing manual labor."

Vera, however, wasn't going to let the matter drop. "Nonsense," she said, turning to Colette. "It would be an honor. Your mother's collection is far too valuable and, more importantly, sentimental to be mishandled. Best for it to be taken care of by those who understand the delicacy of vintage tulle."

Rosemary had to hand it to her: Vera always managed to get what she wanted, particularly when French couture was involved. She possessed charm in spades, and Colette accepted the offer with a grateful nod. Frederick looked as though he might like to protest, but when Rosemary threw in with Vera, and Imogene and Pippa followed suit, he found himself outnumbered.

Of the women, only Ruby refrained from offering her assistance. "I'd offer to help, but my sweetheart needs his good-luck charm by his side. Don't you, darling? Yes, you do."

Rosemary didn't know what was worse: Ruby's constant pouting, her breathy delivery, or the deliberate way she manipulated Mr. Pennington into letting her do whatever she wanted—including tearing down his mansion—a mansion he loved if the enthusiasm he'd displayed while leading the tour was any indication.

"Quite right, my dear. Shall we, gents?" Mr. Pennington repeated his invitation to the fourth-floor billiard room, and Ruby followed the men out, but not before Rosemary noticed the fleeting wistful expression that flashed across her face as she forced her gaze away from the wardrobe.

"Thank you," Colette said when the click-clack of Ruby's heels had retreated far enough down the corridor to render her out of earshot. "I can't stand watching that woman circle like a vulture, stripping my mother's legacy to its bones."

Mrs. Russel nodded sympathetically but refrained from agreeing outright with Colette's assessment. "Your mother, rest her soul, made certain nothing like that would ever happen. Her wishes were quite specific, and the terms of her will iron-clad."

"Thank goodness," Colette smirked. "Father won't see

a dime of her money if he doesn't comply. Not that he needs it, of course, but when has that ever mattered?"

Mrs. Russel again remained neutral and ignored the question, instead turning her attention to Rosemary and Vera. "Would you believe one person could amass such a fabulous collection? I came to Jade when she needed some dresses altered before Oscar was born. From that time to this, she never got rid of a single item. Every garment she bought is still here, including her wedding gown and maternity frocks."

"Mrs. Pennington had quite an eye for fashion," Vera agreed. "This is a Charles Frederick Worth design, is it not?" She pulled out a two-piece confection of ivory silk with pale pink chiffon decorations and a sunbeam pattern embroidered into the skirt. "Look at the gigot sleeves and that ruffled bodice. It's so romantic. I remember seeing her in this in one of the portraits earlier."

"It's lovely," Rosemary agreed as Vera continued to peruse the dresses. "One would expect nothing less from the House of Worth."

"Look at this Doucet gown." Vera held up a confection in gold with lacy sleeves and a flowing skirt featuring floral appliqué over a silk chiffon under-layer. "From Worth to Coco Chanel, and I even saw a Florrie Westwood, that's more than thirty years of fashion all in one place. I feel as if I've died and gone to couture heaven."

"All couture pieces are to be showcased before the auction—displayed in their glory for the gathering masses. Then, everything not bequeathed to Coco will be sold, and the profits donated. The preservation of historical buildings, indeed." Mrs. Russel sighed. "If your mother had known what was to become of this place, she'd have done a lot more than banish your father to the fourth floor!"

Colette muttered something about banishing him to somewhere hotter, which Mrs. Russel ignored.

"I've nearly sorted everything," she said, "but there's still quite a bit of work to be done." Despite her efforts, boxes, bins, and crates were stacked everywhere, covering nearly every surface. "Jade kept notes for every party, meticulously logging what she wore to each one, but otherwise, she wasn't what anyone could call organized, though, of course, I ought not to speak ill of my poor dear friend."

"We both know Jade would have wanted you to call it as you saw it," Imogene mused, receiving a narrow-eyed glare from Colette for her efforts.

"Mother had her own way, of course," Colette snapped, her nose in the air, "but I'd hardly think she'd appreciate having her shortcomings pointed out by the staff, particularly when she isn't here to defend herself." She directed her ire towards Imogene, even though Mrs.

Russel had made the comment. Imogene opened her mouth as if to fire back a tart retort, but she stopped when Pippa shook her head sharply.

Mrs. Russel cluck-clucked but didn't admonish Colette, evidently as accustomed to her outbursts as everyone else in the house. "Now, now, dear. Your mother enjoyed her messes with a twisted sense of pride, even going so far as forbidding Mrs. Doon or any of the maids from moving so much as a hairpin while cleaning her closet. She was quite unreasonable, and it won't do to pretend otherwise. To remember her as she truly was is the only way to honor her."

Utter silence followed the comment. Colette couldn't argue the point, or perhaps her soft spot for Mrs. Russel kept her from doing so, but the awkward moment passed quickly, and the mood turned to one of focused efficiency.

"Why don't you come help me wrangle your mother's winter things from the other closet," Mrs. Russel implored Colette, and the two of them set off, leaving Rosemary, Vera, Imogene, and Pippa alone for a serene half hour.

"You weren't exaggerating, were you?" Vera directed the question towards Imogene, but her eyes remained trained on Mrs. Pennington's collection of handbags. "It's like a Shakespearean tragedy in here."

Pippa laughed, a trilling and, for the first time,

genuine sound. "I've dealt with worse, let me tell you. All of my clients are difficult. People with expensive tastes are particular. It's part of the job and means I have to be even more discerning. It's exhausting but rewarding. At least, that's what I repeat in my head whenever Mr. Pennington speaks."

"He's long-winded, that's for certain," Rosemary agreed. "And you weren't wrong about the pompous. I'm just sorry he recognized the Woolridge name. I suppose we ought to have arrived through the servants' entrance after all, shouldn't we?"

Now it was Imogene's turn to laugh. "It would have made Mrs. Doon's day, and we wouldn't want that!"

"And I should have kept my thoughts on the Cassatt to myself. When it comes to art, I tend to become enthusiastic."

Pippa waved away Rosemary's apology. "Imogene is just used to being the person in the room who usually has the correct answer, that's all."

Imogene rolled her eyes at her friend and said with a laugh, "She's impertinent, but she's not wrong." Any lingering tension Rosemary had felt melted away, and it was all too soon before Mrs. Russel and Colette returned with a rack of fur coats.

Vera lost herself among the pelts while Imogene and Pippa set to work pulling hat boxes down from the upper shelves. When they'd amassed a pile nearly as tall as

Mrs. Russel, Pippa climbed off the step stool and carried a pair of boxes to the chaise longue where Rosemary sat untangling beaded necklaces.

They each pulled a lid off one of the boxes, Rosemary discovering a fabulous musketeer hat and Pippa an assortment of items, including a bum roll, a feathered boa, and a leather-bound book. Curiously, she opened it, her eyes searching the pages for a short moment.

"Oh, it seems to be a diary," she said, closing the cover with a snap. "My apologies." Before the words left her lips, Colette snatched the book out of her hands.

"Those are Mother's private thoughts," Colette snapped. "She'd be mortified to know some stranger had read them."

Again, it took a considerable effort for Imogene to bite her tongue, and before she could have second thoughts, Rosemary cut in and said gently, "I'm sorry, Colette. It can't be easy to watch veritable strangers sort through your mother's things. It must feel like your memories are being stripped away."

Colette didn't answer because she hadn't been paying any attention to Rosemary's apology. She'd been flipping through the diary pages and must have read something she didn't like because her face clouded over, and for a moment, it looked as though she might let loose a barrage of tears. She stuffed the diary into the pile of items designated as sentimental, and just as quickly as her facade had cracked, she put it back together.

Rosemary's heart softened infinitesimally. It had been fleeting, but for a moment, there had been a human being underneath Colette's tough facade. She might be a pill, but she had recently lost her mother and was now expected to welcome a woman like Ruby Snow into the family—as her stepmother, no less. Not many people would be able to endure the situation with any aplomb. Suddenly, Imogene's one-dimensional assessment of the heiress felt unduly harsh, although Rosemary could understand the inclination to take her at face value.

"Your mother truly did possess exquisite taste," Vera said, her love of all things related to fashion coming across in her near-worshipful tone, and coaxing, if not a smile, at least something less surly than a scowl from Colette. "All of these beautiful pieces and then an original Jeanne Lanvin to top it off? I'm simply dying to see it."

Mrs. Russel smiled at Vera. "It's meant to be on display before the auction, but unless Coco objects, there's no reason why you can't see it now if you'd like. Were you planning to attend?"

If Colette objected, she declined to say so out loud.

"Not if my husband, Frederick, has his way." Vera tilted her head and gave Mrs. Russel a wink. "But I know how to get around him."

"I've no doubt on that score. Now, we'll need to clear a path to that armoire against the back wall. I left the Lanvin hanging in there for safekeeping this morning when I began sorting, and now it's buried."

"That's quite all right," Pippa assured Mrs. Russel. "We'll have this organized in a jiff."

Mrs. Russel smiled gratefully and then turned her attention back to Colette. "Dear, are you certain there's nothing here of sentimental value?" she asked, indicating a long rack on wheels that sagged beneath the weight of too many perfectly fashionable yet exceedingly sensible frocks. They were just the type a lady of Jade Pennington's station would be expected to wear to somber affairs such as Sunday service or meetings of the Daughters of the American Revolution.

Colette declined with an offhand, "None of those were truly her style, nor are they mine. They were an obligation, one she might have embraced for the sake of her reputation, but an obligation nonetheless. I'd prefer to remember her dressed for a party, wrapped in the finest silks and shimmering with jewels. Best to let them go and give the money to the preservation society. It's what she wanted."

Pippa volunteered to clear some space by dispensing with the rack. "If they've already been labeled, I'll take them down to the portrait gallery and log them for auction. None of them look special enough to be put on display."

Colette spun around, her eyes narrowed to slits and landing on Pippa. "They might not have been Mother's style, but all those dresses are of the highest quality, and each one is probably worth more than you make in a month. She wouldn't have appreciated your impertinence."

Imogene's patience had worn thin, and she snapped, "What she wouldn't appreciate is the way you repeatedly speak to people as though they're beneath you." Even after the words popped out of her mouth, she showed no remorse. Pippa's face seemed to be caught somewhere between a grimace and a grin, as if she couldn't help herself from enjoying the way Colette's nostrils flared indignantly. "Jade cared about her reputation and enjoyed her place at the top of the social hierarchy, but she also recognized that it was a fleeting, arbitrary system and not an excuse to look down upon others."

Instead of apologizing, Colette stuck her nose in the air and resumed rummaging through the wardrobe. Her actions represented a type of person Rosemary simply couldn't abide. She was a hypocrite; she could dish out insults all day but ran from real confrontation. Mrs. Russel refrained from commenting and also continued about her business, but when her back was turned, a look of disbelief passed between the rest of the women.

It didn't take long to reach the armoire with so many helpers, and when they did, Mrs. Russel paused for a last dramatic moment before throwing open the doors. "Oh my stars!" she exclaimed in unison with Colette and Vera's twin gasps. "It's gone!"

Indeed, the armoire was empty, and Mrs. Russel was beginning to get worked into a tizzy. "It's impossible! I know it was right there this morning. I saw it with my own two eyes!"

Chapter Eight

Mrs. Russel ascended the stairs at a clip Rosemary wouldn't have thought possible given her age and stature and stormed into the billiard room in a tizzy. Ruby snapped up to standing from her position bent over the billiards table, the coy smile sliding off her face to be replaced by a thin-lipped frown.

"It's gone! Mrs. Pennington's prized couture gown—the pièce de résistance of the display—crafted by Jeanne Lanvin herself, stolen right from under my nose! It's a travesty, a crime, I tell you!"

"Now, now, Mrs. Russel," said Mr. Pennington crossly once he understood what she was going on about. "Let's not be dramatic. It's only a gown, after all, and it isn't as though Mrs. Pennington will be missing it."

Colette let out something resembling a growl at the comment, causing her father a moment of pause. His eyebrows drew together in a rare show of contriteness.

"That isn't what I meant, dear, of course. I only intended to imply that it must be somewhere around here; if it isn't, it simply won't be part of this unseemly auction. Surely, one missing piece of frippery isn't the end of the world, is it?"

Mrs. Russel shook her head emphatically. "I'm afraid, sir, it wasn't slated to be part of the auction at all. It was only meant to be displayed because your wife willed it to her daughter as part of Coco's inheritance."

Again, Mr. Pennington seemed poised to object, but Mrs. Doon appeared in the doorway. "I wouldn't dismiss the concern so cavalierly, sir. That gown cost more than Miss Colette's coming-out party. If poor Mrs. Pennington isn't rolling over in her grave, it's because she's on her way back to haunt the house!" she exclaimed, making the sign of the cross.

"I suppose it's good that this place is being torn to the ground. Before long, she'll have nothing to haunt but rubble." The deadpan declaration came from Ruby, and even Mr. Pennington stared at her, stunned.

"You unbelievable witch!" Colette exclaimed, raising one pale, impossibly thin arm in Ruby's direction. "It was her. She stole the Lanvin. Isn't it obvious?"

Ruby, whether to her credit or detriment, remained calm and refused to rise to the challenge. Colette's ire seemed to roll straight off her back, causing Rosemary to wonder if such indifference was an inherent trait or a form of manipulation Ruby had been forced to cultivate. The woman continued running her fingertips over Mr. Pennington's forearm and merely watched as her future stepdaughter built up a head of steam.

"Coco, darling," her father wheedled, having recovered quickly from Ruby's insensitive comment, "you don't honestly believe she would do such a thing, do you? What reason would Ruby have to pilfer from your mother's closet? If there's something she wants, she can merely have another made. Surely you can see how unnecessary it would be to steal?"

Mr. Pennington's tactic of asking questions that included the only acceptable answer grated on Rosemary's nerves. After presumably having been forced to answer them all her life, Colette was far less patient.

"Surely," she spat back, "you can see that you might not be the only thing of my mother's your little trollop covets? It wasn't enough for the two of you to insult us from the other side of the park. You had to bring her here, and there must be a reason. Women like her don't do anything—certainly not men like you—for nothing."

The insult fell like a stone, and the entire room was rendered speechless once more. Even Finn wore a disappointed frown, though he might have been the only one who expected more from Colette.

Aghast, Mrs. Russel exclaimed, "Why, I never!"

Mrs. Doon sneered. "Of course you have. You've been with the family even longer than I have, and you know that girl has never been expected to behave like a member of civilized society.

Ruby recovered quickly and somehow snuggled even closer to Mr. Pennington. "Someday when you're older," she said to Colette condescendingly, "you'll understand the appeal of a mature, sophisticated man. There isn't a woman alive who could resist your father's charms. He can be quite persistent when there's something he covets. Can't you, darling?" She made a cooing noise that seemed to particularly scandalize Mrs. Doon, who let out an audible gasp.

Still hardly ruffled, Mr. Pennington said to Colette, "I know you're upset, darling, but I must insist you keep your wits about you. We'll find this whatever-it-is, and all will be well. Please don't take it out on Ruby. It's not her fault. Tell her, darling. Tell her you wouldn't do such a thing."

As ordered, Ruby turned, pinning her gaze on Colette for a long moment before glancing pointedly down at her own ample bosom, then back up.

"We were...of different sizes. Your mother didn't own a dress fit to show off my greatest assets."

Beside Rosemary, Vera stifled a snort of laughter while Colette's face went from pale to deep red, which Ruby either didn't notice or chose to ignore. "This house has been full of people all day," she said offhand. "Anyone could have nipped up there and stolen the dress. My money is on one of the staff, and which one of them had the most access? Why, Mrs. Russel, of course."

Mr. Pennington's gaze landed briefly on Ruby with something resembling irritation for the second time that day. Rosemary wondered if she was the only one to notice the woman had finally spoken in a tone that didn't come off as kittenish, then decided she wasn't alone after glancing at Oscar's stormy expression. He regarded his father with an expectant frown, but Mr. Pennington clamped his mouth shut.

Mrs. Russel opened and closed hers several times before Colette scoffed in her defense, "That's absurd!"

"Agreed," replied Mrs. Doon. "I'm afraid the only way to solve this is for nobody to leave until we've found the gown. Mrs. Pennington would be distraught if she knew."

"She would. And more so if she knew Mrs. Russel had been blamed." Imogene patted Mrs. Russel on the shoulder.

Oh, dear." Mrs. Russel laid her hand briefly over Imogene's. Now that the adrenaline had evaporated, her shoulders slumped, and she looked more diminutive than ever.

Frederick, already bored stiff before the perusal of

Mrs. Pennington's closet had forced him into the billiard room, had become even less thrilled as the afternoon wore on. It was only due to the impending promise of nine glorious innings from directly behind the dugout that he'd endured it with any affability, and now his irritation boiled over. "What, precisely, do you mean to say?"

Mrs. Russel, not intimidated by Frederick in the least, drew herself up to her full if insubstantial height. "A thief has been invited into this house. There's no other explanation, and nobody leaves until we figure out who is behind this horrible crime."

"I appreciate your predicament, Mrs. Russel, but quite frankly, I don't give a damn," Frederick retorted, Mr. Pennington's habit of refilling everyone's drink the moment it emptied, having rendered his lips fairly loose. "Frisk me if you must, but unless I'm smuggling this whatever-it-is beneath my trousers, I think it's safe to say I'm not the culprit—and neither are my friends."

"Of course you aren't," Mr. Pennington replied in a voice Rosemary didn't entirely believe was meant to soothe, and Leo stepped in front of the door in case the culprit tried to flee. "Certainly, nobody suspects an upstanding businessman—a Woolridge—of pinching something right from underneath our noses. Unless, of course, you're not who you say you are." He stroked his chin thoughtfully. "How do I know your presence at this time isn't an elaborate ruse? If this gown of Jade's is as valuable as I'm being led to believe, anyone might have reason to acquire it and deceive us to do so."

Rosemary half expected her brother to become combatant, but not for the first time did he surprise her by instead remaining quite calm—so calm it was almost disconcerting. "If you have a question regarding our credentials, I'll be happy to call my father's solicitors over on Seventh Avenue." He rattled off the name of an esteemed firm with offices in both London and New York. "Surely you'll trust we are who they say we are?"

Mr. Pennington peered at Frederick for a long moment. "I don't think that will be strictly necessary," he finally admitted. "I would, however, humbly request that you stay while a cursory search is performed. It would make Mrs. Russel feel more comfortable. What do you say?"

Vera, who would prefer to linger, patted her husband on the arm. "It's a Lanvin, Freddie. I did so want to see it, and it will be a travesty if it's not found. I must help if I can." She fluttered her eyelashes, and Frederick was a goner. Not even the great Babe Ruth could have convinced him to refuse his wife, so he agreed to Mr. Pennington's request with a reluctant nod.

"If we all search, we'll find it that much faster." Frederick didn't need to add that the sooner the gown was found, the sooner he could escape, but the thought was written all over his face.

"She's not being left alone," Colette said, her gaze pinned on Ruby. "I don't want her anywhere near Mother's rooms."

Mr. Pennington sighed. "Have it your way, Colette," he said, using her full name for the first time without an endearment. His voice was sharp, but it sounded more like resigned disappointment than anger to Rosemary. "There are plenty of us to go around; we'll split up into pairs and each search one floor. Ruby and I will take my rooms on the fourth level if it suits you."

"Perhaps Mrs. Russel ought to accompany you, Coco," Oscar piped up. "I'll search the galleries on the second floor since I know those rooms the best."

Finn took the opportunity to reprise his role as Oscar's champion, suggesting, "Miss Langley seems the natural choice for your partner, doesn't she?" He also employed Mr. Pennington's question habit, though without Colette's sarcasm, leaving poor Pippa little choice but to agree.

"With all the closets, we'll need more than just us two up there," Colette said, catching Vera's eye first and then Rosemary's. Her gaze flicked towards Imogene, indicating she'd prefer their company to hers.

Before Colette could say any more, Imogene bowed out. "I'll take the ballroom. It's full of items for the auction, and I'll know better what's in each of the crates.

One of you strapping gentlemen can help me with the heavy lifting."

Desmond needn't have jumped so quickly to attention, as neither Frederick nor Finn had any intention of fighting for the right to overly exert themselves, and with that, it was settled. Desmond would join the object of his affections on the second level, and to Frederick's relief, he and Finn would search the ground floor where, with people in and out all day, the priceless gown was least likely to be stashed.

When Mrs. Doon volunteered herself and Leo to search the servants' quarters on the top floor, Leo looked less than pleased with the assignment, but it was Ruby who balked. "You trust them alone, yet I need a chaperone?" She appraised Mrs. Doon with disdain.

This time, Oscar didn't hesitate to speak up, earning himself a grateful smile from the maid. "Everyone here is innocent until proven guilty. Why don't we all simply focus on our assigned areas."

"Very well. Come, darling. We'll scour every inch of your bedroom," Ruby replied, tugging Mr. Pennington along behind her.

Chapter Nine

Colette and Vera performed a search of the library before retreating to the family bedrooms on its north side; Rosemary and Mrs. Russel focused their efforts on the seldom-used south-facing guest suites. The Pennington mansion was full of nooks and crannies, innumerable trunks, cupboards, and chests where one gown could have been stashed, and it felt quite like searching for a needle in a haystack.

And while Rosemary appreciated Mrs. Russel's commitment to thoroughness, she moved far more quickly and could cover twice as much ground in half the time. "I'll just pop over to the next bedroom, then." Rosemary figured she could be finished in there before Mrs. Russel was through searching beneath the bed.

Without Mr. Pennington chattering in her ear, Rosemary found herself rethinking her appreciation for modern architecture. No one could fault Jade Pennington's taste in decor, only her penchant for excess, which was concentrated mainly on the floors where she had once entertained guests.

Rosemary wondered why Jade had felt the need to fill the place with so many possessions. Was she more concerned with wealth and status than Imogene realized? Or had she been trying to fill a hole to compensate for something she felt was missing from her life? According to her daughter, Jade Pennington had never wanted for anything, but perhaps Colette didn't know all of her mother's secrets.

Every few minutes, Rosemary checked in on Mrs. Russel. On her way through the sitting room, she heard a noise coming from the direction of the staircase—a choked scream followed by a loud thud.

An intense wave of déjà vu followed by a cold sense of dread propelled Rosemary towards the landing. She knew it wasn't simply the sound of shoe boxes tumbling to the floor this time, and she wasn't the only one who'd heard the cries. "What was that?" Vera asked when she and Colette caught up, each wearing the same concerned expression.

"Ahhh—ack," came another garbled moan.

Even though it no longer resembled that of a young, innocent ingenue, Rosemary recognized the voice of the person in distress before she flew through the double doors into the library.

Sprawled across the great ornamental rug where, just

a couple of hours before, Mr. Pennington had made a great show for his betrothed, lay Ruby, and for a split second, Rosemary wished she hadn't run so quickly. She had thought stumbling upon dead bodies was unpleasant, but watching someone take their last breaths—even someone as loathsome as Ruby Snow—was far worse.

She convulsed and contorted, eyes wide and wild, hands clutching at her throat. An angry red rash had risen up her neck and across her face, and her mouth bubbled with a foamy substance that could only mean one thing: poison—a fatal dose, from the looks of it. Instinctively, Rosemary mentally cataloged every detail of the scene before Mr. Pennington arrived and shoved past her forcefully.

"Ruby! Ruby, darling! Oh no. No, no, no!" He scrambled to the floor next to Ruby and attempted, unsuccessfully, to help her. "Someone do something, then! Call the doctor now!"

Mrs. Doon, who had been staring at Ruby with her mouth agape and her eyes filled with sadness and pity, came back to attention and indicated she would carry out Mr. Pennington's orders. Within a few moments of her departure, all the light had drained from Ruby's eyes, and then, after one last gasp, she was gone.

Mr. Pennington gathered her into his arms and let out a wail that sounded as pained as Ruby's last and lingered even longer. Although Rosemary understood his inclination to scream, she kept a clear head and focused on the assembled group's faces. By now, the entire household had filtered in, forming a semicircle around the dead woman, each staring at her corpse. Ruby was striking even in death, though probably not in the way she would have preferred.

Standing across from her, Rosemary noticed Imogene's gaze following the same pattern hers had traveled only moments before. When their eyes met, Imogene gave an almost imperceptible nod, which Rosemary returned. She was certain had there been chance to speak, their thoughts would have run on similar tracks.

Oscar's skin paled to practically transparent, Finn looked as though he might be sick at any moment, Pippa as well—they'd both turned a miserable shade of green—and Colette wore an unfathomable expression. If forced to comment, Rosemary would have said she appeared just as shocked as everyone else, save Mr. Pennington's man, Leo, who maintained the same grim half sneer as usual.

"Someone's poisoned her," Colette declared, breathless and wide-eyed, stating out loud what everyone was already thinking. She wasn't wrong; someone had hated Ruby enough to want her out of the way for good—enough to stop simply fantasizing about doing it and to put desire into action. However, Colette might have waited for a more appropriate moment to mention the fact.

When Mrs. Doon returned to the library with cheeks rosy from the effort of so many trips up and down the stairs and announced breathlessly, "The doctor is on his way, and so are the police!" Mr. Pennington seemed to come to his senses. He'd stopped moaning, but it still took Oscar, Finn, and Imogene to peel him away from Ruby's side. During the ordeal, her hands fell away from her neck, revealing a blotchy red puncture wound below her left ear.

With the attention on getting Mr. Pennington settled into one of the settees by the fireplace, Rosemary seized the opportunity to take a closer look. She smoothed Ruby's hair back into place, closed her eyes, and gently tilted her head to one side. Sure enough, it wasn't a birthmark or a blemish; Ruby had been pricked with a sharp, round object—most likely a needle, but Rosemary knew better than to make assumptions.

"Coco's right. This was no accident; someone poisoned her. But how? Wasn't she with you?" Oscar shook his head sadly and peered at his father with concerned eyes.

"We—well, she—Ruby said she needed to freshen up," Mr. Pennington stuttered. "She was in the powder room for quite some time, so I set off alone to search."

Rosemary felt another pang of empathy for the man,

followed by a swift change of heart. She couldn't help but think that if Colette's insinuation regarding her father's infidelity was true, Mr. Pennington had merely reaped the suffering he'd sown. And yet, he looked as though he'd aged a decade since entering the library, and the pendulum of Rosemary's emotions swung back in the other direction.

"Looks like someone's chickens have come home to roost." Colette spoke in a low tone, but still, her voice carried.

"Is this what you wanted, then?" All the fight had gone out of Mr. Pennington's voice. "Are you happy now? Have I been sufficiently punished?"

Colette held his gaze and refused to back down. Rosemary couldn't imagine addressing her own father in such a way, and certainly not in front of guests. It was an intrusion, being there, privy to private matters and family secrets, yet nobody could look away.

"Only God knows who has paid proper penance for their sins," Colette replied finally. "It isn't me you need to convince—although, it seems you're running out of people to whom you can apologize."

Mr. Pennington paled, and Mrs. Doon gasped loudly. "Surely, Miss Colette, this discussion can be continued later." She nodded pointedly at the assembled group of strangers, but her admonishment didn't accomplish its desired goal.

"You'd do well to remember your place, Mrs. Doon," Colette spat, "if you want to keep your job."

Mrs. Doon waved a hand as if swatting at a fly. "I've heard it before, and I'll hear it again, I don't doubt, but it's not you who I take orders from, is it? What do you think you'd do if I weren't here to see to the household, I ask you?"

"I suppose you should be glad I consider the running of this place none of my nevermind," Colette retorted.

"Just when I was beginning to feel sorry for that girl," Vera said under her breath after the Penningtons resumed bickering.

"Coco, that's enough," Oscar said over the din, for once sounding sure of himself. "Stop terrorizing the staff. Mrs. Doon has a point; you're embarrassing yourself and the entire family." Colette opened her mouth to retort but her brother cut her off. "Leo, please help my father to his room. He needs to rest, wouldn't you agree?"

Leo strode across the floor, taking Mr. Pennington by the arm and attempting to escort him as instructed. "Yes, of course. He's had quite the shock. Perhaps a sedative will do him good."

"I have had quite the shock, but I'm still standing right here, and I don't appreciate being referred to as though I'm not in the room," Mr. Pennington admonished. His eyes flicked back to Ruby's prone figure and filled with a fresh supply of grief. "I'm not…I can't…I can't leave her," he stuttered, stared and then, after a long moment, seemed to realize there was nothing more to be done. Abruptly, he stopped talking and allowed Leo to lead him out of the library and up to his rooms.

"Mrs. Doon, how long did the police say they'd be?" Oscar asked once his father had gone.

"Not long, but she's already passed, so I suppose it won't matter if they don't rush." Her eyes widened, and she apologized immediately. "Oh dear, what am I thinking? That was insensitive. I suppose I've had a bit of a shock as well."

"We've all had a bit of a shock, Mrs. Doon," Oscar said gently, "and the afternoon isn't over yet. I expect we'll spend the rest of it recounting every nuance of the day to the police. There will be an investigation, and we'll all be under suspicion. Rightfully so, I suppose. There's a murderer amongst us." He sounded perplexed rather than accusatory, as though he couldn't quite believe the words were true.

"He's right," Imogene agreed. "Someone—one of the people in this house—killed Ruby. The wound on her neck suggests she was injected with some form of poison."

"Not just any form of poison," Colette piped up. "It was atropine, wasn't it?"

She directed the question towards her brother, who sighed and nodded. "Naturally."

"And how do you know that?" Pippa asked, earning herself an eye roll from Colette.

"I'm a Pennington, of course. It's the family business. And as such, I'm happy to say I have an alibi for the time Ruby was murdered. I was with her." Colette gestured in Vera's direction. "Isn't that right? We weren't out of one another's sight, not even for a moment."

"That's correct," Vera answered without hesitation.

"And I was with Fred there, in the morning room, searching for the gown," Finn explained quickly.

Frederick's tone turned to one even his closest friends hardly recognized when he asked, uncharacteristically seriously, "That's not strictly true though, is it?"

Finn started almost the same way he had when Imogene had asked what he did for a living, and again, Colette seemed poised to speak for him, but before she could, he smiled sheepishly. "I suppose not strictly speaking. We did sneak over to Mr. Pennington's smoking room, but that was quite a while before Ruby—well before we heard her hollering. Certainly, you would agree with that?"

"Yes, mate, on that, I can agree. Quite a while before, indeed, and we were together except for a few moments when you used the loo. I didn't intend to cast aspersions, only to speak plainly. Beating around the bush does nothing but create confusion in these types of situations." Frederick ought to know, given he'd once been wrongfully suspected of and even charged with murder, but he was no fool and kept that fact to himself. "I, for one, will admit to having only cursorily searched the salon before wandering into the smoking room and um…admiring Mr. Pennington's Babe Ruth autographed baseball collection."

"I'm curious how Ruby slipped away from the fourth floor in the first place," Pippa mused. "And why would Mr. Pennington let her? What could he have been doing?"

"Surely you aren't suggesting that my father had something to do with this?" Oscar asked incredulously, springing to Mr. Pennington's defense. "He's positively distraught. Anyone with eyes could see that." For the first time, he looked as though he might not be entirely enamored of her.

Contrite, Pippa backtracked deftly. "Of course he is. I wasn't making light of his grief. The point is, she was here on the third floor when she was supposed to be up on the fourth with your father. Perhaps she was looking for or meeting up with someone—maybe her killer."

"Or maybe she was coming back to retrieve the Lanvin she stole," Colette suggested.

"Coco, honestly, if I hear the word Lanvin one more time—" Oscar stopped short of stating what he might do, perhaps having decided midway through the exclamation that making threats, even idle ones, was unwise given the circumstances.

Colette ignored the warning. "That gown was priceless, and Ruby certainly proved she wasn't above taking things that belonged to someone else. Husbands, dresses, what's the difference? She made plenty of enemies, is all I'm saying. None of the staff would have worked for her even if Ruby had asked them, not even dear Mrs. Russel, with her unending patience. I believe she even threatened your position, Miss Langley. Tell me, did you stick to my brother like glue during your search?"

Taken aback at being questioned, Pippa sputtered, and Oscar quickly stepped in to speak for her. "We were together the entire time, except when I declined to follow her into the toilet," he said dryly, receiving a grateful nod from Pippa that, under normal circumstances, might have rendered him speechless. "Neither of us could have sneaked upstairs, administered the poison, and then returned to the second floor; it's not possible."

"That's right," Pippa agreed, "there simply wasn't time."

"Well, quite frankly, it doesn't make any difference to me either way. Personally, I just want the Lanvin back. Ruby can rot, for all I care."

Chapter Ten

Ruby's body was taken away out the back of the mansion so as not to draw more attention than necessary. The police insisted upon detaining the household for questioning, just as Oscar had predicted they would. Now, they were all seated in the spacious morning room, surrounded by Mrs. Pennington's extensive collection of antique tea sets. Rosemary would have given anything for a good cuppa right about then, but unlike the chipped, throwaway cups used at Imogene's speakeasy, these were exquisite bone china never, ever actually used to consume tea—and certainly not bathtub gin!

Several deputies milled about under the direction of Detective Maguire, a harried-looking man with guarded eyes and an impatient expression.

Mr. Pennington had been administered a sedative and was ensconced in his room, but his man Leo had come back down and now stood sentinel over the proceedings. Colette didn't bother to suppress an eye roll at his self-important expression. "How does it feel to have your nose firmly implanted in my father's—?" Oscar interrupted her with a loud clearing of his throat, and she stopped talking, instead focusing on her cuticles.

Rosemary couldn't help but replay the conversation from the library in her head. The people with the most to gain from Ruby's death were the Penningtons themselves, but Colette's reminder that Ruby had alienated the staff was also valid. Truly, only the infatuated patriarch had actually wanted his fiancée there.

The tragedy of the fact was lost on Colette. "Are we nearly done here?" she complained, ignoring the detective's disapproving frown. "This unpleasantness has left us all feeling rather drained, and I, for one, would like to lie down for a while."

Detective Maguire raised a brow. "This unpleasantness, as you put it, is the loss of a human life, Miss Pennington. I must insist that you treat the situation with the gravity it deserves."

"If you'd known her, you would surely agree the world is a better place without Ruby Snow." Colette appeared utterly unintimidated by the detective's tone or implication, or by her brother's exasperation.

"Please pardon my sister's impertinence; she doesn't know what she's saying. Shock, you know." Oscar spoke up in Colette's defense. "Her relationship with the deceased was rocky at best, but Coco wouldn't hurt a fly. She's far more bark than bite."

"Yes, well, most poisoning victims are surrounded by friends and family who insist they'd never stoop so low." Detective Maguire paused a moment to let the implication sink in. "We'll follow every lead, of course, starting with the type of poison used. Isn't atropine the key ingredient in your father's company's latest drug? Do you use Bella-quil, Miss Pennington?"

He made the statement offhand but caught Colette's gaze and held it.

Oscar's expression hardened. His gaze flicked between his sister and the detective, and before she could reply, he answered instead. "Certainly, Coco has access to Bella-quil, as does everyone else in this house. Atropine is wildly misunderstood; it alleviates quite a number of symptoms and, if taken at the recommended dosage, is perfectly safe."

"Safe, you say? Interesting," mused the detective. "In small amounts, it does aid in digestion, reduce hay fever symptoms, and when applied topically even alleviates joint pain, but in higher concentrations, atropine causes a hot, dry rash, convulsions, and cardiac arrest. Was Miss Snow known to have taken it habitually?"

Oscar remained quite calm and shrugged. "I certainly don't have the faintest idea what Miss Snow's health regimen might have included. It wasn't any of my nevermind, was it? Perhaps she unwittingly mixed too many of the wrong pills." The submissive tone had gone out of his voice to be replaced with the hint of a challenge, and his spine was straighter than Rosemary had observed before.

Even Pippa, who hovered next to Imogene in the opposite corner of the room, appeared affected by the shift, her gaze curious as it lingered over Oscar for a fraction of a second longer than usual. Yet, despite his dismissive explanation, Mrs. Doon continued to regard Colette with suspicion, as unmoved as Detective Maguire.

"Yes, perhaps."

"Maybe she did us all a favor and took them on purpose," Colette mused, causing her brother's cheek to twitch once, even though he refrained from looking at her directly. "Wouldn't that just be the berries?"

Rosemary didn't think for one second that someone as vain and with as many aspirations as Ruby would bump herself off, and if she had, it seemed more likely she'd have ensured a more glamorous exit than the one she got.

Detective Maguire wasn't buying what Colette was selling, either. "Wouldn't you consider it irresponsible to keep so much of a potentially dangerous substance in the house?" he pressed.

Colette had the gall to let out a tinkling laugh.

"Almost anything can be a dangerous substance in the hands of the right individual," she said, renewing Rosemary's vow to refrain from trying one of Mr. Pennington's miracle pills no matter the circumstances. "And before you ask, the answer is yes. I had reason to visit the library some time before Ruby keeled over, but I wasn't alone. Vera here will verify that we never laid eyes on that tart while we were in there."

"I saw her," Mrs. Doon clapped a hand over her mouth as if she hadn't intended to speak.

"Miss Pennington?" The detective attempted to clarify. "In the library?"

"No," Mrs. Doon shook her head vehemently. "Ruby, Miss Snow that is, and not in the library. It was earlier in the day, in the gallery. She was talking to Mr. Finn, and it looked like they didn't want anyone to catch them at it." Mrs. Doon cast a sly glance in Colette's direction. "Sneaking around, I'd say. Up to no good, the pair of them."

"Shut up, you old cow." Colette glared at the older woman. If looks could kill, the detective would had had a front-row seat to a second murder.

"I'm only saying what I saw."

"I said, shut up." But this time, Colette's attention focused on Finn with a certain amount of speculation.

"Colette, that's enough," Oscar said sharply. "Don't you suppose you've pried everything you're going to get out of my sister?" This he directed towards the detective who, after an extended pause, nodded and waved a hand to dismiss Colette.

She turned on her heel and marched out of the breakfast room, slamming the door behind her. The temperature rose a degree or two when she'd gone, but it plummeted again as Detective Maguire resumed his interrogation.

"Mrs. Doon, you and Mr. Sterling were both unaccounted for at the time of Miss Snow's death. Is that correct?" he asked patiently, his face impassive. "You and the remainder of the servants, that is."

The maid's veneer cracked momentarily, but she drew herself up to her full height and stuck her nose in the air. "Unaccounted for? We were doing our jobs, weren't we? I myself was all the way up on the fifth floor, searching the servants' quarters. You can ask Madeline. She's one of my girls. I spoke to her just before I heard poor Miss Snow's cries."

"Mmm hmm," came the detective's noncommittal reply. In contrast to his earlier method of pelting questions, now he merely allowed silence to goad his target. Rosemary rather appreciated the show of versatility and filed the technique away for later employment.

"Surely you're not insinuating that I might have killed Miss Snow?" Mrs. Doon seemed to find the suggestion utterly absurd.

"I'm not insinuating anything, simply gathering the facts, but it's interesting you should jump to that conclusion. Now, you said you were all the way up on the fifth floor, but Miss Snow's body was found in the library..." He left the statement hanging in the air for a long moment.

Mrs. Doon stared and sputtered, "Four other people have already admitted to being in the vicinity, including Miss Colette. That girl has done nothing but spit insults and accusations ever since her father announced his engagement. She had more of an ax to grind than I do."

"Surely, Mrs. Doon, you're not also pointing the finger at my sister?" Oscar asked archly, his tone far less polite than any he'd used before when speaking with the maid. "She's been through enough, losing her—our—mother so abruptly. I know the two of you have had your differences, but you've watched her grow up. You can't truly believe Coco would do such a thing."

Mrs. Doon stared at Oscar, and her mouth opened and closed a couple of times before she averted her gaze. "Of course, I think it's highly unlikely that Miss Colette would actually follow through on her threats, but you have to admit she has been the most vocal about her feelings towards Miss Snow. She would have suffered the most with Miss Snow as a stepmother. Perhaps you don't know what that sort of thing can do to a girl, but it's enough of a motive in any case."

"Colette was right about one thing, Mrs. Doon. You should tread carefully," Oscar warned, his tone eliciting surprise from the maid.

A tense silence followed the statement until finally, as if the heated exchange hadn't happened and even though he'd observed every detail with his hawk-like gaze, the detective said, "We'll need to speak to Mr. Pennington, of course, and get his side of things."

Mr. Pennington's man lost his internal battle then and spoke up indignantly, "Certainly, you don't expect Mr. Pennington to sit through an interrogation at this time? My employer is distraught. Furthermore, he wasn't anywhere near Miss Snow when she was—er—when she died. I saw him upstairs in his rooms on the fourth floor right before she screamed, and then I followed him down the stairs. So, you see, he can't have had anything to do with it."

Mrs. Doon nodded in agreement. "That's right. I saw Leo following just behind Mr. Pennington as I came down from the servants' quarters."

Detective Maguire nodded, thanked Mrs. Doon for her time, and dismissed her from the room before taking statements first from Imogene and then Pippa. They each described their whereabouts and what they'd heard and seen until the detective was satisfied.

"Thank you, ladies. You may go."

Judging from the reluctance on her face and the speed of Imogene's steps, she'd have preferred to stay, but Detective Maguire waited until the door had closed behind her before jotting down a few more notes.

Next, he asked Rosemary for her whereabouts just before the death.

"I see," he said when she had finished her succinct retelling. "And you were with Mrs. Russel the whole time?" The detective glanced at Mrs. Russel, who had remained silent during the entire ordeal, her face tipped low from the shock of it all. "Is that how you remember it Mrs. Russel?"

He had to repeat the question before she looked up at him. "Why, yes." Then she bit her lip. "I was with Miss Rosemary on the third floor in the guest wing when the commotion broke out." Her eyes filled with tears, and she began to shake. "I'm sorry, it's just that I've never been witness to such a tragedy."

Confronted with an elderly woman sobbing her heart out, Detective Maguire resorted to chivalry and dismissed Mrs. Russel. When she'd gone, he repeated the question to Rosemary.

"That's right. We were together when I heard Ruby call out and ran to see what the matter was, and well…the rest you know."

Nodding, Detective Maguire made a few more notes,

then looked at Rosemary, his eyes boring into hers. "And you are willing to state, for the record, that you both were in constant contact the entire time?"

Rosemary opened her mouth to assure him of exactly that, then realized it wasn't technically true. "Except for a few minutes when we each searched one of the bedrooms in the double suite, but Mrs. Russel would have seen me go past the door as they were both open at the time."

"So then you were separated from Mrs. Russel, at least for a spell."

Rosemary kept her tone as neutral as possible even though, just below the surface, her blood roiled indignantly. "Yes, I suppose I did break away from her, but only briefly. I'm certain she'll corroborate that I was never more than a whisper away."

Detective Maguire nodded and wrote another note in his book. "And you said Mrs. Russel was quite convinced someone had stolen a—what is it?—a gown worth several thousand dollars? A gown she was, for all intents and purposes, responsible for?"

"Well, yes," Rosemary agreed, "but I hardly think that has anything to do with Ruby's murder. Mrs. Russel is a frail, elderly woman," Rosemary replied. "It's utterly ridiculous to believe she managed to sneak away without me noticing, or that she could have overtaken Ruby to administer the poison even given the opportunity." What admiration Rosemary had felt towards Detective Maguire's investigative prowess quickly waned as she attempted to defend such a ludicrous suspect.

"You'd be surprised what someone of her station might do for a few thousand dollars," he said placidly, and Rosemary suddenly became even more incensed than she had been before. It wasn't her who he suspected—it was sweet little Mrs. Russel!

Rising, Rosemary took several steps towards the door.

"A theft and a murder occurring within hours of one another?" Detective Maguire's voice followed her, rising as she twisted the knob and opened the door a crack. "It doesn't take a genius to put two and two together, does it?"

"Was there anything else you needed to ask me?" Rosemary's voice could have frozen the ears off a brass donkey. "Or am I free to go?"

"Not at this time. However, if, as you say, she wasn't in your line of sight for some moments, I'll need to ask Mrs. Russel a few more questions."

Furious, Rosemary wanted to slam the door behind her, but didn't. Instead, she pulled it gently shut and walked away, oblivious to the fact that Imogene stood behind a potted plant near the door, her eyes burning.

Chapter Eleven

All of the effects of Mr. Pennington's generous pour had been burned off with the adrenaline rush following the discovery of Ruby's murder, rendering Rosemary and the rest of her friends quite sober indeed.

When Imogene asked, "Does anyone fancy a drink?" Desmond didn't dare answer for the group and instead looked to Frederick, who merely shrugged and said, "I'm a cork on the waves. A drink sounds like just the ticket." A murmur of agreement settled it, and when they arrived, it was a relief to discover the Monday night crowd had mostly dissipated.

Imogene consulted with Tuesday and tended to some business, then settled them all into a secluded table in the back and said, "The Italian restaurant down the street does a wonderful chicken parm. I'm sending Zeke out for takeaway."

"Genie told me what happened," Tuesday said apologetically when she returned to the table. "It sounds like you all could use a treat, and you've come to the right place. I've just finished concocting tomorrow's special."

Chuffed, Frederick said enthusiastically, "Consider us your willing test subjects." It turned out her concoction was a delicious, sweet and tart punch made with copious amounts of rum that went down smoothly and eased some of the day's tension.

When they'd nearly finished eating (the food was just as good as Imogene had promised), Desmond finally asked, "So, what do we all think about this murder business?" He addressed the group as a whole, but his eyes flicked between Rosemary and Imogene.

Imogene wiped the marinara sauce from her fingertips and sat back in her seat. "I think more people wanted Ruby Snow dead than alive."

"You took the words right out of my mouth," Rosemary agreed. "I've never seen a case with such a clear and obvious motive. Truly, everyone had a reason for wanting Ruby out of the picture, and not only that—they all had the means. Anyone who's set foot in the Pennington mansion has been offered a dose of Bella-quil. They practically give it out at the door like party favors."

"And yet," said Imogene, "it seems nobody could have done it. We were all partnered up; everyone in the house accounted for at the time of her death, with very little opportunity to sneak away."

"It's an impossible problem," Frederick lamented, "and I know this will be an unpopular opinion, but why don't we simply leave the whole sordid business to the police and be on our merry way?"

"The police are welcome to solve this case all on their own," Rosemary said with a shrug, "but that doesn't mean we'll be able to wash our hands of it. For one thing, Imogene has to go back there to finish preparing for the auction. For another, we always say we'll stay out of it, and yet we always get pulled back in."

Imogene agreed. "Ruby Snow was pretty much exactly the person Colette accused her of being, at least at first glance. I didn't care for her, but she was murdered in my friend's home. Turning a blind eye isn't an attractive option."

"Then it's settled. We're at least going to have to try to sort it out—for our own satisfaction, if nothing else. And it's not an impossible problem, Freddie—there's no such thing. Ruby was injected with the poison; she didn't keel over of her own volition, no matter what Colette would like to believe. Just because they all seem to have alibis doesn't mean they didn't do it. It simply means—"

"—that someone is lying," she and Imogene finished the sentence together.

Desmond nodded slowly. "Or two someones. If

nobody sneaked away from their partner, both halves of one of the pairs would need to be in on it together."

"That's a good point, Des."

"I do have the occasional clever thought, you know."

"Of course, it looks worse for the couples who were on the same floor, and out of that group, it's quite obvious which one wanted Ruby dead the most—Colette."

Rosemary wanted to point out that the most obvious suspect was usually innocent, but before opening her mouth, she remembered one of her late husband Andrew's favorite lessons: nine times out of ten, it was better to listen than to talk. She had always teased that his math was wrong, insisting the ratio must be closer to 70/30, but either way, she decided to allow Imogene to lead the conversation.

"Except she couldn't have done it," Vera said, to Rosemary's satisfaction. "She was never out of my sight, not even for a moment."

"What about you, darling?" Frederick asked his wife. "You've been rather quiet, which isn't like you. Are you all right? Not scarred by the day's events, I hope?"

"Of course not, you silly man," she replied. "I'm simply satisfied in my own opinion and don't feel the need to prove anything to anyone. The truth will come out eventually."

"Whatever do you mean? What's the truth?"

"You won't like it, but my prime suspect is Finn Clark. Now, Freddie, my love, I know you think he's above suspicion, but he tried to get you to cover for him, which means he has something to hide."

Frederick raised an eyebrow at his wife. "There's a flaw in your theory, dear. I'm telling the truth; I honestly don't believe Finn could have done it. We weren't separated long enough, which is why I didn't overly press the issue with the police."

"While I adore you, darling, I do know how distracted you can get, especially when your interest has been caught. Babe Ruth autographed memorabilia and a collection of rare baseball cards? Can you honestly say you know exactly how long the two of you were separated?"

"Would it do any good to say yes and reiterate that I'm positive? I suspect not, although I must say it seems unfair that nobody questions you when you say what you saw but I'm somehow untrustworthy."

Vera ignored the comment. "He's dodgy, that one, confident and quick on his feet. I think he'd do anything to hold on to Colette and to keep whatever secret he's holding under wraps. I only hope she doesn't get hurt when it all comes out."

Imogene stared at Vera. "You actually like that horrible young woman? You don't find her positively abhorrent?"

Unflappable as usual, Vera replied with a shrug. "She's sad. We've met her sort before, haven't we, Rosie?" she asked not waiting for a reply. "Just plain miserable and blaming the world for all their problems, but mostly harmless. Except, of course, on rare occasions." Rosemary guessed her friend was referring to a murder that had taken place at Woolridge House in the sleepy village of Pardington, where they had all been raised. "But I don't think Colette has the stomach for murder. Not really."

Rosemary agreed. "Perhaps, perhaps not. One never knows, but I don't disagree. She strikes me as someone who desperately desires the approval of everyone she encounters: friends, family, and virtual strangers. It's an impossible expectation, one doomed to disappoint and result in bitterness, but one she isn't solely responsible for creating. And, it doesn't make her a murderer."

Imogene huffed out a snort. "Are you seriously suggesting I ought to feel sorry for Colette Pennington, a filthy rich heiress who has been so spoiled for her entire life that she feels the need to throw a temper tantrum every time she doesn't get the attention she thinks she deserves?"

"Of course not," Rosemary said calmly. "I'm merely pointing out that she's not much more than a girl and one who recently lost her mother. Unfortunately, grief wears many faces and can make already ugly people even uglier. She's managed to alienate nearly everyone, save Mrs. Russel. The woman is a saint."

"Speaking of which, that Detective Maguire rubbed me the wrong way. He seemed to have it out for Mrs. Russel," Imogene said, swirling the whiskey around in her cup. "What was that about?" She asked the question lightly, but Rosemary couldn't help but feel a lot was riding on her answer.

Rosemary's face darkened. "He's an absolute lout; he actually tried to insinuate that Mrs. Russel might have had reason to steal the Lanvin and murder Ruby! I reiterated that I'd been no more than a whisper away, and I don't think he appreciated my description of his theory as *utterly ridiculous*."

The explanation seemed to appease Imogene, and she nodded, the tension ebbing.

"He sounds like the kind of guy I'd serve a sneezer at the bar," Tuesday commented.

"A sneezer?" Rosemary asked, her expression of disbelief teasing a grin from Tuesday. "As in sneezing in his drink? You mean to say servers really do that?"

"Sure do, more often than you'd suppose," she replied, "though I certainly can't imagine you doing anything to warrant that kind of retaliation."

Rosemary wasn't entirely certain she wasn't being placated, and it irked. "How positively satisfying. I can think of a few people whose drinks I'd enjoy sullying," she said, rather enjoying Tuesday's look of surprise at the comment. That would teach her to make assumptions, Rosemary thought, feeling vindicated but not entirely sated.

Tuesday laughed throatily and said, "I like this one. She's got spunk."

Imogene nodded in agreement and smiled, though it didn't quite reach her eyes. It was Vera who replied, winking at Rosemary and saying, "She's got it in spades. Don't let her fool you."

"My money is on Mr. Pennington. It's always the least obvious suspect—the one who seems to have the thinnest motive." Frederick leaned back against the bar, took a swig of his drink, and made the same observation Rosemary had wanted to mention earlier, though not quite in the same context. "Perhaps he didn't want to marry Ruby at all. I mean, honestly, who would?"

"Most men with eyes, I suspect, brother dear, and I hate to say it, but if your money's on Mr. Pennington, I think we can count him out on odds alone."

Frederick shot his sister a quelling look. "You know, the thing about odds is that at some point, I'm going to be right. He rubbed me up the wrong way, just like that detective did the two of you ladies. There's something not quite right about Mr. Pennington, murderer or not, mark my words."

"He's not entirely wrong on that count," Imogene said

thoughtfully. Her immediate acceptance of Frederick's theory chafed, given how quickly she'd shut down Rosemary's comments regarding Colette. Still, Rosemary held her tongue on that count because, ultimately, she agreed with their impression of Mr. Pennington.

"I might be willing to wager a guess at what Mr. Pennington and Ruby were doing not long before her death," she said, allowing the unpleasant details of the discovery of the body to wash back over her. "She smelled of him, if you know what I mean. It doesn't necessarily help solve her murder, but it might explain why he didn't question her lengthy visit to the loo."

"You're not surprised, are you?" Imogene wanted to know. "It's common knowledge that they were together since well before Jade passed away. Mr. Pennington isn't the only one in the family needing *constant attention*."

Rosemary wasn't surprised, of course, not after Colette's insinuating comments, but she was grateful for the confirmation and also for the opening to ask a question she'd been wondering about ever since Ruby had turned up dead. "Was there anything suspicious about Jade's death?"

Imogene's eyebrow rose to her hairline, and she sighed. "No, there wasn't. We spoke shortly before she died regarding her estate. She'd received a grim health diagnosis and knew she wasn't long for this world. Now, I wish I'd pressed her for details, but the tabloids had been rumbling over Mr. Pennington's blatant infidelity, and I didn't want to pry."

"I'm sorry for your loss, Imogene," Desmond said, patting her on the arm.

His sympathetic tone seemed to knock the emotion out of her as fast as it had risen to the surface, and Imogene declined to reply. Instead, she said, "Jade was the best of them all. She treated everyone, including her staff, respectfully and didn't look down on others for their social status. I can't say the same for the rest of the Penningtons. They're all obsessed about their reputations." Imogene huffed as though there was no trait more unbecoming. "The entire family is suspicious. It stands to reason one of them had the most to lose if Mr. Pennington married Ruby—and they also have the most to gain by her being out of the picture."

"The entire household is suspicious, not just the Penningtons," Rosemary insisted. She couldn't help but feel that Imogene's accusations were one-sided. "Mrs. Doon definitely had her hackles raised. She may not be family, but she lives at the mansion and was forced to endure Ruby on a daily basis."

"Mrs. Doon has been in that house since Colette and Oscar were children. She's loyal to a fault, but that's what paying higher than anyone else on the block will get you—loyal servants. It doesn't mean she would commit murder for them."

"I'm not suggesting she did; I'm suggesting she might have lied. Loyal to a fault, as you say, when there's a paycheck involved—then it's likely she might be motivated to bend the truth, particularly if she thought there might be something to gain by doing so. She was paired with that man of all work, Leo, and it didn't go unnoticed by me that Mrs. Doon hastened to alibi him along with Mr. Pennington."

There wasn't much Imogene could say to refute Rosemary's point, so she nodded. "Perhaps. If I'm being honest, it would give me significant pleasure to discover that old dragon of a woman had offed Ruby Snow, but it just doesn't ring true. My instincts are screaming it's one of the Penningtons."

Desmond nodded along in agreement as if Imogene had stated an irrefutable fact as opposed to her personal opinion, and Rosemary had visions of elbowing him sharply in the ribs.

"Colette, of course, for obvious reasons," Imogene continued. "She's angry, and deservedly so. Then there's Finn, although I can't see what he has to gain other than pleasing Colette. However, as Vera said, he's already acted suspiciously, so it seems he might bear further consideration. Oscar acts aloof, but he's more eager to please than he lets on. He wants to deserve his father's praise."

Her tone niggled at Rosemary's nerves, as did her insight, but even so, Rosemary couldn't help pointing out, "I don't think killing Mr. Pennington's betrothed would accomplish the task, nor would it help the Pennington family image. Furthermore, haven't we already determined that if one half of the partnered couples is lying, the other one must also be? Oscar was paired with Pippa," she said, letting the insinuation hang there for a long moment, "which, of course, is preposterous."

Imogene had stilled between the two comments, her face set in hard lines. With an effort, she unclenched her jaw and said, "Preposterous would be one word for it. I have every faith in Pippa."

"I don't think Rosemary intended to imply anything about Pippa." Vera made an attempt to smooth things over.

"I suppose not." Imogene didn't seem convinced.

Finally, the evening drew to a close, and Frederick, of all people, begged off. "We'd better get some sleep and make tomorrow worthwhile; after that, I'm afraid I'll be tied up with work. I did come here to do a job, after all."

"I almost forgot you had one," Desmond replied smoothly. "Frederick Woolridge: responsible adult. Doesn't quite roll off the tongue, does it?"

"We can't all be layabouts forever," retorted

Frederick. "After all, there are chairs to be covered across the world, didn't you know?"

"Oh, about that, Freddie," Imogene said, the corner of her lip twitching. "I'm terribly sorry to have dragged you to the Pennington mansion. I'm even more sorry I dropped you smack in the middle of a murder investigation, and I know you're rather disappointed at having missed the Yankees game, so I asked Tuesday to pull a favor and arrange a little surprise for you."

Frederick perked up like a puppy who'd caught a whiff of steak, his eyes sparkling. "You don't mean?"

"Box seats," she said, smiling widely. "We'll all go, even Pippa, if that's all right with all of you." The delivery of the comment seemed to catch Rosemary off guard. She thought perhaps there was a hint of a challenge in the statement but shook off the notion. "She's as bad as Tuesday; she's married to her work and won't take a day off unless forced. Is everyone in?"

None of them would have dreamed of dashing Frederick's hopes, so there was only one answer to that question.

CHAPTER TWELVE

"Freddie, if you keep grinning like that, someone will think you're a madman. Don't your cheeks hurt?" Rosemary ribbed the next day when they arrived at Yankee Stadium, and his eyes lit with youthful delight. She had to admit, the stadium was impressive. The hot dogs smelled heavenly, the sun was warm on her cheeks, and the buzz of excitement surrounding her first American baseball game was palpable.

Rosemary had spent most of the night lying awake and replaying the end of her conversation with Detective Maguire in her head. By the time she finally fell asleep, she was certain Imogene had heard just enough to conclude she had been trying to convince the detective that Mrs. Russel was guilty of murder. No wonder Imogene had turned cold so quickly. With an effort, Rosemary shook her head to relieve the unpleasant thoughts and tried to have as much fun as her brother.

"Aaaaand strike two!" the announcer boomed. At

least, that's what Rosemary thought he said. It all sounded like gibberish through the loudspeaker.

The crowd went wild, and when pressed as to why, Frederick explained, "It's a three-two count, meaning the pitcher has thrown three balls and two strikes. One more ball, and the hitter walks; one more strike, and—"

"Heeeee's outta there!"

"That one I got," Rosemary said with a smile, which grew into one of welcome when Pippa arrived and took a seat in the stands.

Imogene had been right about Pippa being married to her work. She greeted the group warmly, but her expression quickly turned to one of worry. "What is it?" Imogene cajoled.

"I'm supposed to be at work, keeping my nose to the grindstone. The auction is still scheduled for Friday, and everything has to be set on time. That's less than two days! When I called the house this morning, Mrs. Doon informed me Mr. Pennington was in no mood to receive guests." Pippa scowled at the memory. "She didn't say outright he'd prefer the people under investigation for his fiancée's murder weren't traipsing around the house like vultures, but she might as well have done. Except we aren't guests; we have a job to do."

"We'll get everything ready in time, Pippa, don't fret," Imogene assured her. "And don't worry about Mr. Pennington or cranky old Mrs. Doon. They have to let us follow through with the terms of Jade's will, whether they like it or not."

Pippa smiled thinly. "That's true. It's imperative that the auction goes smoothly—not only for the sake of Mrs. Pennington's memory but for my job as well. Although, with Ruby out of the picture, I suppose I've got a better chance at keeping it."

Rosemary's ears perked. "Why is that?" she asked with interest.

"Well," Pippa said, looking around as if to ensure nobody was listening and realizing belatedly there was no need, "she certainly didn't like me. She didn't like anyone besides Mr. Pennington, and even then, how she spoke to him always felt like an act. Nobody talks like that; it was all for show. Better actresses than Ruby have played the innocent ingenue, but, of course, Mr. Pennington couldn't see the nose on his face. She was poison, and her death a fitting end."

Perhaps Pippa's paranoia hadn't been misplaced after all. Her exclamation had drawn Desmond's full attention and one of Frederick's eyes away from the game; he still had one trained on the field, but she had caused him some pause. Pippa stopped talking and gasped. "I should not have said that."

Vera tugged the brim of her hat a little lower to protect the tip of her nose from the blistering sun and waved a hand to dismiss Pippa's concern. "The damage is already done, I'm afraid. No use not speaking candidly, and wouldn't it be worth it if it turns out you know something useful that helps solve the case?"

"My wife is merely justifying a deep-seated need to engage in all forms of gossip." Frederick tossed the comment over his shoulder, watching while a fly ball whizzed into the crowd behind third base. "Lucky duck," he said when one of the men who'd been standing there came up out of the seats with it triumphantly grasped in his hand.

"How and why did Ruby pass judgment on you?" Vera asked, waving her husband away and returning to the conversation with avid interest.

"Oh," Pippa replied with a start, "you didn't know? Ruby got wind of Oscar Pennington's little crush on me." At that, Pippa's cheeks pinked slightly. "And advised Mr. Pennington to have me fired. She didn't know I was in the next room, and I heard her say it wouldn't be right for his son to marry someone of my station—as if her last name was Rockefeller! She wasn't born on the Upper East Side, I can tell you that."

Imogene let out a snort of agreement.

"Anyway," Pippa continued. "Mr. Pennington told her it was just a silly infatuation and that when I finished with the auction, Oscar would forget all about me, which, quite frankly, would please me to no end. Not that there's anything wrong with him, of course," she hastened to add, her cheeks pinking, "but Mr. Pennington is likely quite correct, and then I'd be out of a beau and a job! Plus, he's odd—attractive enough, but odd all the same."

Rosemary heard the hint of a question in Pippa's voice, as though perhaps she didn't think him so odd after all, only she wasn't certain why. Vera caught her eye and winked, proving Rosemary's hunch was not entirely off base. If anyone could spot a crush from a mile away, it was Vera. She doubted, however, that Imogene would approve of the match, and her theory was verified a moment later.

"You don't have to apologize for not fancying a man like Oscar Pennington," Imogene said, attempting to close the subject. "Even his mother worried about him. She said it was a constant battle to ensure he didn't end up like his father. What does that say about him?"

For some inexplicable reason, Rosemary hesitated. She wondered what exactly Imogene meant by *a man like Oscar Pennington*. Her disdain was beginning to feel personal, given there were more similarities between Rosemary's family and the Penningtons than between them and Imogene.

Furthermore, Jade's description of her son seemed off to Rosemary. So far, she'd seen Oscar act with a sensitivity that Mr. Pennington didn't possess. "Do you suppose she meant to imply he's also a philanderer?"

Imogene shrugged. "Perhaps. She never said anything so blatant. I took it to mean that he's a wolf in sheep's clothing, which would track with the infidelity. Perhaps he and Ruby had a thing going on the side."

If that were true, Rosemary could understand Imogene worrying over Pippa. She was protective, and she meant well, but did that mean Jade Pennington's opinion could be taken as gospel truth? The woman might have been a fashion icon and the head of the society set, but most considered her eccentric as well. If she was more worried about Oscar than Colette, perhaps she hadn't been an astute judge of character. Except, Rosemary couldn't very well say that in front of two of Jade's biggest fans, so instead of pressing, she changed the subject and put her brother on the spot.

"What about it, you two? You were alone with the lot of them in the billiard room. Did it seem as though Ruby had her sights set on Oscar?"

"Well, she was a bearcat, certainly," Frederick said, his attention too focused on the field to answer all of his sister's questions. It was only the bottom of the second inning, but the Yankees had already scored one run, and there were two men on base. "No dumb Dora, despite the coyness, but she couldn't have cared less about Oscar. Of course, that could have been a cover-up, but it doesn't wash for me. Eyed old Des here for a few minutes longer than necessary when Mr. Pennington wasn't looking, though."

Desmond's eyebrows shot towards his hairline, "She did not," he protested, his eyes flicking to Imogene. That he didn't understand Ruby's attention would do more to improve his position than harm it was precisely why Rosemary worried he would end up with a broken heart.

"Yes, she did," Frederick insisted. "Don't misunderstand; I'm certainly not insinuating she would have taken it any further than that, but I also wouldn't say it was out of the realm of possibility, given what I know about women like that."

It was Vera's brow that lifted then. "Would you care to elaborate on precisely what you *do* know about women like that, dear husband?"

Without turning around, Frederick replied smoothly, "If I were daft enough to answer that question, you wouldn't have married me in the first place."

Imogene's eyes had flicked between the couple with amused curiosity, Frederick's reply bringing a smile to her lips and seeming to answer a question regarding the nature of their relationship.

"What about you, Vera?" she asked. "What did you make of Ruby Snow? I suspect an actress such as yourself—an observer of human nature—would have a fascinating opinion regarding our controversial leading lady."

Vera leaned forward in her seat, the baseball game

merely a backdrop as far as she was concerned. Frederick and Desmond both attempted to pay attention to what she was saying for a few short moments, but when the Yankees shortstop caught a line drive and went careening towards second base to make a double play, they gave up the pretense.

"I certainly got the sense that everything that came out of Ruby's mouth had been carefully constructed and cultivated," Vera said carefully. "She was guarded, as though she was always playing a role. I doubt she even knew who she was anymore, deep down. She may have been the billboard we perceived her to be, or she might have been wildly misunderstood. It seems we'll never know."

The loudspeaker boomed, cutting into Vera's insightful, if not theatrical, description of Ruby. "And that's the end of the fourth inning, folks! The Yanks are ahead by two runs with the Tigers up to bat!" Rosemary understood what the announcer had said this time, and she took some pride in the fact. "Get your peanuts, get your popcorn! And then get back to your seats. You won't want to miss a pitch!"

"And that's my opportunity to use the loo," Frederick said, and Desmond quickly made to follow. "Would you ladies like anything from the concession stand?"

"You won't have time for both," Imogene warned. "There will be a line, so you should expect to be gone a while."

Vera stood up, stretched her legs, and offered to retrieve snacks, leaving Rosemary, Imogene, and Pippa alone in the stands. For a scant handful of minutes, the trio engaged in a spirited debate over which Yankee looked best in his uniform, and then two gruff-looking men pressed into their aisle and plopped down to occupy the empty seats.

"I'm sorry, but those are taken," Rosemary explained politely.

"Yeah, they are, aren't they?" One of them dismissed her with a roll of his eyes.

Rosemary turned on the wheedling tone that had so often proved effective in convincing men to do her bidding. "But we have tickets."

"We don't care what ya got, sweetheart," the other one retorted, along with a lewd statement suggesting where Rosemary could shove her tickets. Her mouth fell open in surprise, and she felt Imogene tense beside her.

She leaned forward past Rosemary to address the men directly, nostrils flaring. "Are you deaf or just blind and stupid? My friend said these seats are occupied. Now, go chase yourselves before I scream at the top of my lungs and draw every eye in the joint. I'm sure there are a few gentlemen amongst the crowd who wouldn't mind sending a couple of palookas like you out of here in a meat wagon."

The men looked like they were working up a protest, but Imogene opened her mouth wide, and they scurried off. "Morons" she said when they'd gone. "Boobs like that need a taste of their own medicine now and then. You really have to give them what for." She mimed a one-two punch and made a popping noise with her tongue.

Rosemary sniffed indignantly. "I was taught you catch more flies with honey, but apparently, nobody in this city has any manners whatsoever!"

"Well," Imogene said with a shrug, "this isn't London or the Upper East Side. Nobody up here cares that you look like little birds help you put on your clothes every morning."

There was an undercurrent to her tone that Rosemary didn't expect—bitterness or perhaps exasperation—and yet she found herself unsurprised. Had she not, after all, predicted that Imogene would have a flaw? Judgmental and presumptuous were two negative marks in Rosemary's book, but Vera returned to the seats with her arms full before she could formulate a reply. Vera handed off a box of popcorn, a bag of candy floss, and a bar of chocolate to Frederick, who followed in her wake.

"You'll be sick if you eat all that," Rosemary warned.

"Shush, and listen to this." Vera rustled open a newspaper she'd been carrying under the sweets. "*Poison on Park Avenue.* There's a whole article about

Ruby Snow's death." Her eyes sparkled at the intrigue.

"Pharmaceutical baron Charles Pennington's new fiancée, Ruby Snow, was found dead on the library rug of his Park Avenue mansion yesterday. Police say the death was ruled a homicide by poison injection and that all leads are being followed. Several suspects are under investigation at this time.

Sources say anyone who knows the Penningtons shouldn't be surprised to discover their treachery. Colette Pennington has few friends left in the society set, and her brother, Oscar, was never part of it, to begin with. Perhaps he has more important things to do, such as run Pennington Pharmaceuticals, while his father is otherwise engaged.

According to sources, Mr. Pennington has been gallivanting about on either side of the park for years. The relationship between him and his late wife was strained at best, but even so, Mrs. Pennington must be rolling over in her grave to know her husband planned to remarry so soon — to a woman the same age as their daughter!

Furthermore, it's been stated that the poison used in the murder was atropine, a derivative of the plant belladonna or deadly nightshade, also the main ingredient in Pennington Pharmaceutical's famous digestive aid Bella-quil.

Best not to joke about arsenic in the teacups, folks, not when you're having luncheon at the arsenic factory."

"Those papers are such rags," Rosemary spat. Imogene cocked her head curiously at the comment.

"Rosie is still angry with the London papers for what they printed about her butler, Wadsworth, when he was accused of murder," Vera explained as if there was nothing out of the ordinary about that at all.

"You have a butler?" Pippa asked, impressed.

Imogene rolled her eyes. "I think the more pertinent question is why was he accused of murder?"

Rosemary explained, as succinctly as possible, how Wadsworth had been found standing over the body of a slain police officer, and it had fallen to her to find and foil the real killer. "Even though I cleared his name, he's still endured more humiliation than any innocent man deserves. It's one thing when it's news, but gossip and hearsay have no place in the press. They treated him as though he was guilty from the start, mostly due to his occupation and social status, and unfortunately, people pay too much attention to splashy headlines. Someone at the Pennington mansion is a murderer, but the rest aren't."

"I applaud your integrity, but let me ask you something," said Imogene. "Is your butler still suffering due to what the papers said, or has the whole debacle blown over?"

"I suppose his life hasn't been changed irrevocably," Rosemary admitted.

"Precisely. The roar will subside once the real murderer has been put to justice. Mr. Pennington doesn't deserve your pity. He's a cad who didn't possess enough self-restraint to abide by the rules of his marriage. A man like him is probably just as duplicitous when it comes to his business. If that's the case, his son would be complicit, presumably. As far as Colette goes, her reputation is already circling the drain."

"In Colette's corner of society, poisoning Ruby Snow might actually improve her position," Pippa replied thoughtfully, evidently having abandoned her previous position against gossip. "Ruby was an even bigger social pariah than Colette is. Still, Colette's not nearly as dim as she likes everyone to believe. She wouldn't be so vocal about hating Ruby if she'd actually killed her; she would have pretended they were friends and then publicly mourned her to drum up sympathy."

Pippa made a good point, one even Imogene couldn't refute. Rosemary had to hand it to her; Pippa was the type to see all and say little. Well, except for now. Rosemary could see why Oscar was interested and hoped for the sake of the pair's budding relationship that he didn't turn out to be the guilty party after all.

Once she got going, Pippa didn't seem ready to stop. "Colette and Oscar both had reasons for wanting Ruby dead, but you know who deserves a closer look? Mr. Pennington's man, Leo. He hasn't been with them for all that long, but it seems like he's wormed his way in deep."

Imogene's eyelid twitched and she shook her head emphatically. "Jade would never have let her family slide downhill the way they have. It's sad to see how much has changed in the short time since she's been gone." She was too guarded to let so much as a single tear show, but it was clear to Rosemary that she missed her friend.

"There's something about Mrs. Pennington that you should know, Imogene, but you won't like hearing it."

"What?"

"And the pitch—it's a strike! But wait, the Tigers' catcher dropped the ball!" The loudspeaker screeched and caught even Imogene's attention.

"Why is he running? Isn't he out?" Frederick exclaimed, confused when the runner made a play for first base.

Imogene smirked. "I suppose it's an obscure rule; it doesn't happen often, and the specifics have changed over the years, but essentially, the catcher can't drop the third strike. Well, he can, but it's treated like a fly ball. If first base is empty, and he can get there before the catcher tags or throws him out, he's safe."

Frederick was used to a woman schooling him—he was married to Vera and brother to Rosemary, after all—and for the most part, it slid off his back, but he had fancied himself an expert when it came to baseball. "Oh, I see," he said lightly, and Rosemary felt a wave of smug satisfaction at the thought that perhaps she wasn't the only one not entirely enamored of Imogene.

Once the men went back to watching the game,

Imogene turned to Pippa. "What were you about to tell me before?"

In the meantime, Pippa had had second thoughts. "I'm not sure I should say anything."

"If it helps us catch a killer, we need to know," Rosemary said as Pippa bit her lip and flicked a look at Imogene before deciding she'd better talk.

"Before Colette ripped it out of my hands, I saw a few lines of that diary, and what I read tells me Mrs. Pennington wasn't as nice as you think."

The chill that came off Imogene made Pippa shiver. "What? You might as well tell me now."

"She wrote something along the lines of, *I know she must be devastated, and I ought not to take pleasure in her pain, but I can't help feeling she's getting precisely what she deserves.* It could be nothing, of course, an errant thought. It was her diary, after all, and that's where people admit their innermost thoughts—especially the ones they're ashamed to say out loud. I'm sure we've all felt similarly at one time or another."

Her words were meant to soothe, but Rosemary could see that Pippa's revelation had affected Imogene more than she would care to admit. Suddenly, she didn't feel so smug, but there wasn't time to think of something to say to defuse the situation because the game ended, and the crowd went wild.

CHAPTER THIRTEEN

The journey back from Yankee Stadium, located all the way up in the Bronx and quite far from midtown Manhattan, was interminably long and filled with what sounded to Rosemary like a play-by-play recap of what had already been an exceedingly tedious game. If you asked her, there was far too much standing around in baseball, waiting for one man to throw a ball at another man with a stick. It lacked the panache of cricket or the elegance of polo. Still, Frederick was over the moon about it, so Rosemary kept her opinion to herself and instead watched out the window of the elevated train while the neighborhoods flashed by.

"We're closed on Tuesdays, but ironically Tuesday is the only one who doesn't ever seem to need a night off. She'll be behind the bar, I'd wager, mixing up tomorrow's special if anyone's interested."

Rosemary wanted nothing more than to fall into bed, but she agreed to one drink and, when they arrived, discovered she was glad she had. It was one thing to see the Red Door when the lights were low and the party was in full swing, quite another with an empty dance floor and the chandeliers fully lit.

Now, she could appreciate the pattern of the pressed-tin ceilings and enjoy the eclectic decor. On the walls, abstract paintings shared space with Victorian landscapes and an assortment of jigsaw puzzles—some with pieces missing—that had been glued together and framed. She was even delighted by the shadow boxes filled with the pinned and labeled skeletons of small animals and insects. None of it was anything that would have been displayed at the Pennington mansion, that was for certain.

Frederick, however, did not share his sister's enthusiasm. "It isn't the same without the band," he lamented but perked at the sight of Tuesday, who stood amid a pile of crates behind the bar, stashing bottles of alcohol into the space beneath the floorboards. She looked somewhat frazzled, her hair sticking up at odd ends. Imogene rescued a pile of teacups from tumbling to the floor, and Tuesday grimaced. "I'm sorry. I've got to make room back here. It's an utter disaster."

"You should have come, Tuesday. It was an excellent game." Frederick attempted to sway the barkeep. "We had fantastic seats, and we won! On a grand slam, no less. Incredible!"

When Tuesday still appeared skeptical, Frederick threw his hands up. "You're hopeless. Regardless, I had a lovely time. What was that dropped third strike rule again?"

Imogene explained, and the conversation took a technical turn for long enough to nearly sedate Rosemary and Vera. Finally, the men noticed their drooping eyes and took pity.

"Come on. I'll spring for a cab," Desmond offered. Outside, he and Frederick thoroughly enjoyed flagging one down, and it was only after everyone had piled in that Rosemary realized she'd left her handbag inside the speakeasy.

"It's due to the rum, no doubt. I'll just pop back and fetch it. I won't be a moment," she insisted. The taxi driver tossed her an exasperated frown, but Desmond quelled him with an assurance of doubling whatever the meter read at the end of the ride.

Rosemary made her way back towards the entrance to the Red Door, but when she arrived in the courtyard, she heard the idling of an engine echoing from somewhere close by. She couldn't say why she felt compelled to walk to the corner of the building and peer around, but when she did, she discovered the source of the sound.

The vehicle sat quite low to the ground on a set of larger-than-normal wheels and was shaped like a car at the front but had a wide rear portion that reminded her of a coach or an odd lorry. The exterior appeared armored, as though the driver thought they might be shot at while driving. After a moment of consideration, Rosemary realized the notion might not be out of the realm of possibility, for there was no doubt about it: this was an illegal alcohol delivery—just the type of event that might require a quick getaway!

Deciding it might not be worth what was in her handbag to be caught witnessing such an exchange, Rosemary ducked out of sight around the side of the building, repositioning herself in a vantage point where she could watch but not be seen.

Zeke leaned against the exterior wall next to the door, peering around surreptitiously while two other men unloaded boxes from the rear of the vehicle. The younger one, who, from Rosemary's vantage point, looked to be no older than fourteen or fifteen, handed a box to the elder one and said, "That's the last of it."

He peered at Zeke with some interest and, after his companion had disappeared with the box, lit a cigarette and asked, "So, do you know the story of little Timmy?"

"That's the oldest trick in the book," Zeke replied without looking up, "and I'm not falling for it."

The young boy took a long drag and scoffed. "You don't know, do you?"

Zeke finally looked at the boy directly, shifting into a standing position, and said, "I don't want to know, and neither should you. Anyone who truly knows what happened to little Timmy or big Johnny or medium-sized Larry is either dead or will be soon enough. You'd do well to remember that, keep your nose to the grindstone, and get the hell out of this business at your first opportunity. Trust me on this one, kid."

The boy looked as though he might argue, but the set of Zeke's jaw and the deadly serious expression on his face had him thinking twice. Either the temptation was too much to take, or the kid wasn't very bright because he balked anyway and asked, "What do you know about anything, ya chump?"

"Plenty," Zeke replied, "but more importantly, I know enough to keep my head down and my nose clean. Enough to know to stay as far away from your boss as I possibly can."

Rosemary remembered Desmond's explanation of Zeke's past: he'd grown up in the neighborhood, lost his father and two brothers in the war, then followed another brother into the gangster life until Imogene had pulled him out of it all. Carting prohibited booze into an illegal nightclub didn't seem like pulling him out to Rosemary.

"Mr. Pritchett ain't all that bad," the boy retorted.

Zeke shrugged. "Believe what you want, kid. He's a goon. Don't come crying to me when you end up getting blown down by the chopper squad. You're nothing to him, just a body and a means to an end. When you've outgrown your usefulness or become a liability, he'll dispose of you without a second thought. Just like he probably did Timmy."

"I'd be a goner already if not for him and this job," the boy said, but he sounded significantly less certain than before.

How could someone like Imogene—intelligent, capable, insightful—be involved with a man like the boss Zeke described? Rosemary understood why Desmond had offered her the money, and although she'd applauded Imogene's refusal of the funds then, now she couldn't help but wonder if there was another, more worrisome reason. Was Imogene more involved in this life of crime than Desmond knew? Did she enjoy it? How could her conscience let her stand by when children were being corrupted?

Rosemary shook her head. It wasn't any of her business, and suddenly she couldn't stand one more minute in the place. But when she spun around to retrace her steps back to the cab, there stood Imogene, holding her handbag and watching her while she watched the delivery go down.

"It could be worse. At least I don't bring it in in coffins."

Rosemary stepped forward to reclaim her handbag, her hands raised in surrender. "I wouldn't presume to judge your life or your choices."

Imogene smiled thinly. "I may have been born at night, but it wasn't last night. You can't fathom a set of circumstances that would deposit you here," Imogene twirled a finger in the air to punctuate her point, "or indeed anyplace where you don't come off looking practically perfect in every way."

The statement was like a slap to Rosemary's face. She supposed there might have been some truth to it, but there was also truth in her retort. "Isn't it a smidge hypocritical to accuse me of judging you while in the same breath making assumptions regarding *my* opinions?"

"Perhaps, but you clearly aren't the actress of the group. Your opinions are written all over your face. Can you really deny it?"

Rosemary crossed her arms and stubbornly refused to respond to the question, instead saying, "I've bent the rules before—even broken them on occasion—but only ever in the moment and when faced with limited options."

"And that's exactly my point. Your baseline is the high road because that's where you began in the first place, but it wasn't doubloons my archaeologist father was digging for, and he didn't own a company or come from money. He and my mother had love, and one another, which was fine, but it didn't put food on the table."

"Money doesn't solve everything either, you know. It didn't keep my brother from dying in the war, did it? It didn't keep me from becoming a widow far too soon. My life hasn't been full of sunshine and rainbows. We all have difficult decisions to make and crosses to bear. I know that just as well as anyone else. What makes it so much nobler for you to have come from less fortunate beginnings?"

Imogene sighed. "I didn't say it did, nor did I say you hadn't experienced pain or loss. I only said it isn't fair for you to judge the result of my choices without knowing what options I was presented, to begin with."

Before she had a chance to think it through, Rosemary retorted, "No matter the circumstances, I would never put profits and personal gain ahead of what's right."

Imogene shook her head and said with more than a trace of bitterness, "Personal gain? Does it look like I'm getting rich off this endeavor? I'm constantly in danger of being arrested and sent to jail just because I don't think the government ought to have any say over our drinking habits—a sentiment with which you agree if the number of G&Ts I've seen you consume *in my illegal establishment* is any indication. Should I have walked away and let this place go to seed? Do you think it would stop Lucas? The man would sooner put a knife in your back than scratch it, even if he owes you a favor. Believe it or not, I try to do my part to help the people around here—Zeke, who by most standards wouldn't be considered employable, for example. My moral compass may not be pointed as due north as yours, but I do have one. I don't expect you to understand, but I do what I need to do to get by."

Rosemary might have, under normal circumstances, been able to recognize the truth of Imogene's words, but unfortunately, she had indeed consumed a number of cocktails and was too tired and half soused to think clearly. "Is that what you told little Timmy?"

"Who?" Imogene asked, confused.

"Indeed. I'll see you tomorrow." Uncertain who had actually gotten the last word, Rosemary tucked her handbag underneath her arm and returned to the street where Desmond waited impatiently near the cab.

"What took you so long? We had to go up to triple the fare to keep the driver from leaving you here."

Vera had fallen asleep on Frederick's shoulder while Rosemary had been away, but she roused long enough to call attention to Rosemary's sour expression and ask, "What's wrong, Rosie?" before nodding off again.

"Yes, Rose, what's wrong?" Desmond chimed. "Didn't you enjoy today's outing? It was considerate of Imogene to get us tickets to the game, wasn't it? Isn't she wonderful?"

When Rosemary didn't answer, merely mumbled a noncommittal "um hmm," his brow furrowed. What did he want from her, anyway? She could admit she'd been skeptical about meeting Imogene from the beginning—perhaps even reluctant, though she hadn't admitted as much to Desmond. And yet, when they arrived in New York, she'd been pleasantly surprised to discover she'd been wrong about the woman. It wasn't until after Ruby's death that she felt like things had gone sideways between them.

"I knew you'd get along smashingly. The two of you are alike in many ways: you both like to help people, and you both have a mile-wide soft streak that you'd rather no one ever see."

"How very astute, Desmond." Frost tipped the edges of Rosemary's tone, and Desmond finally noticed.

"What? You don't like Imogene?"

"I didn't say that."

"What are you saying, then?" Desmond refused to back down. "Under the tough exterior, Imogene is a deeply sensitive woman."

With deeply unfortunate timing, the taxi passed below a bright streetlight, which illuminated Rosemary's scowl. "I'm sure you see her that way."

"Just give her a chance, Rosie. She'll come round." Desmond's tone indicated it was the end of the discussion and that approving of Imogene was the only acceptable position she could take—a conclusion Rosemary had already made all on her own.

Chapter Fourteen

During breakfast the next morning, Rosemary made a concerted effort to get out of going to the mansion, but every one of her protests was met with Desmond's rebuff.

"Something must be terribly wrong when the esteemed lady detective is not interested in returning to the scene of the crime. Don't tell me you're scared, Rosie, because you usually prefer to be right in the thick of the action. Now, I know you have no desire to follow Freddie to work or tag along with Vera to her callback audition, so what is it then?" His voice carried an edge of warning.

Since there was no way to explain herself without telling Desmond about the confrontation she'd had with Imogene—something Rosemary hadn't fully processed herself and was loath to discuss—she told a white lie, assuring him with less regret than she typically might have felt, "No, not at all. I'm simply anxious to see more of the city, but there's plenty of time for that."

Pinning an innocent look on her face and ignoring Vera's disapproving gaze from across the table, Rosemary managed to convince him. Desmond allowed the subject to drop, and although he didn't let on that anything was amiss during the drive uptown, he wasn't as blind to Rosemary's fib as he pretended to be. Desmond wasn't the only one who recalled Andrew Lillywhite's sage advice on the subjects of listening and observation. When he and Rosemary finally met up with Imogene on the footway outside the mansion, he continued the charade while noting his two friends' unease.

"It's perhaps not the best time for you to be here," Imogene explained. Her expression was strained, and her eyes were cool when they landed on Rosemary but not nearly as frosty as she'd expected. "Mr. Pennington is understandably upset, thundering around shouting at every little thing. The household is in a tizzy. He thinks one of the auction house staff killed Ruby—which extends to the two of you and, of course, Frederick and Vera. He tore Pippa to shreds this morning, and I'm glad I wasn't there to see it. I'd be out of a job and in need of bail money."

For a glorious moment, Rosemary thought she might have been granted a reprieve, but Desmond wasn't prepared to walk away so easily. "We'll take our chances, Genie," he said and pressed inside. It only took a few moments for him to realize she hadn't been exaggerating.

The mansion buzzed with excitement and an underlying tension even more palpable than the one between Rosemary and Imogene. Mr. Pennington's mood hung like a pall over the house, a dark cloud that spanned all five floors and even seemed to have worked its way into the carpet fibers. Rosemary wondered if tearing down the entire house would be enough to clear the sense of doom.

Mrs. Doon seemed to be everywhere as she gave orders to the maids, one of whom carried a tray.

"That won't do at all. Take it back to the kitchen and this time, do it right. Mr. Pennington prefers his sandwich cut on the diagonal. Not from top to bottom. He's in enough of a state without serving him a plate of food he won't eat."

The maid nodded her chagrin and returned the way she'd come, her steps slightly more mincing than before.

"You, there." Another maid froze when Mrs. Doon's finger pointed in her direction. "It's fresh sheets we'll be needing for Mr. Pennington's bed. Don't pay him any nevermind when he argues that he doesn't need them. It was always the same, even when he slept downstairs with the missus. The man would steep in his own filth if I let him."

Off went another maid to do her bidding. This one looked more worried than the last.

Seeing the maid's expression, Mrs. Doon muttered, "She'll never manage. If you want a job done right..." The sentiment trailed off as she followed behind the maid, turning sideways to avoid bumping into Oscar as they passed each other.

"Oh, hello," he greeted Imogene and her friends so politely it almost sounded sincere. "You've returned, I see. My father won't like it—not one bit. But, if you're lucky, you won't have to see him. He's corralled in his rooms for now, but he won't stay cooped up long—fingers crossed he remains relatively sous—er, sedated—until the auction staff has vacated. We would all prefer to avoid another *uncomfortable incident*."

Desmond's eyebrow quirked, and Imogene's face clouded over once more. To Oscar, she replied tightly, "Yes, well, your father has been under an excessive amount of stress. It's understandable why he might have lashed out. Fortunately, we'll all be out of his—and your—way soon enough."

The comment did nothing to lift Oscar's spirits. His frowning face reminded Rosemary of a sad puppy. "I can't apologize enough for Father's behavior. Truly, it's unusual for him to act this way. He's quite congenial most of the time. I do hope Miss Langley isn't too upset."

"It would take more than that to ruffle Pippa's feathers."

To see for himself, Oscar followed the trio to the second floor. Upon arriving in the portrait gallery, which served as the auction staging area, Rosemary noted Pippa's tight-lipped expression and concluded that perhaps the encounter with Mr. Pennington had taken more of a toll than Imogene realized. Pippa might not mind catering to difficult customers, but poison on Park Avenue was beyond the pale.

"That pile is for you," Pippa said without looking up from the clipboard in her hand. "There's a list of pieces that still need to be tagged, and—" When she finally noticed who accompanied Imogene, she stood up straighter, and her tone became more formal. "—and the certificate of authenticity for the silver snuffbox is still missing."

"I can't tell you how sorry I am about my father's outburst," Oscar said to Pippa before Imogene could respond. "There's no excuse, I know, but truly, he wasn't in his right mind. He's distraught and convinced whoever poisoned Ruby is an outsider. He can't accept it could have been someone within the household, and he won't see reason. Please, do what you must, and for my part, I'll do my level best to make sure he doesn't bother you any further."

It appeared as though Pippa wanted to reply to

Oscar's reassurance but the words caught in her throat. "It's preposterous, you know," she said finally, to her own and Oscar's surprise. "To think one of us killed Ruby. We're professionals, here to do a job—a job those of us without trust funds actually need."

Oscar looked pained and said stiffly, "I understand, and, of course, we're going to see this event through to the end. Fortunately, it's not Father's decision. If it were, he'd call it quits on the whole auction. However, Mother set this in motion, and for all his bluster, he would never go so far as to betray her wishes."

"Thank you," Pippa replied, somewhat mollified. "It's a lovely collection, and it would be a shame if it didn't fetch as much as possible for the preservation society. It's only too bad they can't prevent this house from being demolished."

"Mother would have appreciated that. I know she had her particularities, the need to amass such a collection, for one. At some point, the collecting itself became the obsession. It gave her pleasure to possess things other people wanted; she would buy things she didn't even like to keep someone else from having them. I don't know what hole she was trying to fill, but I can't imagine she could have fit anything else in there—or in this house. It's full to bursting as it is."

Imogene blanched at Oscar's description of Jade Pennington, and Desmond's brows drew together with concern

Oblivious, Oscar plowed ahead. "I adore this house, but it is ostentatious and far too much space for our family, in my opinion. I'll be quite pleased to have my own place. A modern apartment, perhaps, with clean lines and very little clutter. Simplicity suits me, as long as—"

"As long as there's a view," Pippa said, finishing his sentence. A wide smile spread across Oscar's face, and Pippa cocked her head to one side, leaning towards him slightly. She let out a tinkling laugh, and with it, Rosemary knew she'd been right—Pippa did fancy Oscar; she simply wasn't ready to admit it, not to herself, him, or anyone else. "Who do you think killed Ruby?" she blurted.

Oscar frowned at the bold question, and even Rosemary was surprised at the inquiry, but Colette appeared from around a corner with Finn hard on her heels before her brother could answer. She appraised Pippa with contempt.

"If Oscar knew who did it, don't you suppose he would have told the police like a good little boy?" She was just as coiffed as she'd been the first day Rosemary and her friends had visited the mansion, even though it was quite early in the morning, and she presumably had nowhere else to be.

In fact, Rosemary was beginning to wonder whether

Colette ever left the house, but she supposed Pippa's description of her as a social pariah had something to do with it.

"Coco, stop torturing people," Oscar admonished his sister in a warning tone.

"It's very kind of you to stick up for me, Oscar," Pippa said smoothly, "but I certainly didn't mean to imply that you were withholding evidence in a murder investigation, and I don't need rescuing." She turned to Colette. "I was simply interested in his opinion, but evidently, that's above my station."

Colette ignored the comment with a shrug, then diverted her attention to her cuticles and adopted a bored expression. "Whoever killed Ruby did us all a favor," she said. "I wish I *could* take credit for it."

Oscar's expression turned as stormy as Rosemary had ever seen it, and he snapped, "When will you learn not to speak every thought that goes through your head? The only thing Ruby's killer did was to ensure she'll never be gone. Had Father simply been left alone to see her for what she was on his own, perhaps he would have fallen out of—"

"Here now. Take care how you speak to your sister." Finn jumped to Colette's rescue.

"He knew what she was, Oscar," Colette said impatiently, "he just didn't care, and you're even worse than he is if you see it any other way. Father will move on; he moved on from our mother, didn't he? And they were married for twenty-odd years. At that rate, he'll have forgotten about Ruby before the ink on her death certificate is dry."

"Enough of this." Oscar put a hand on his sister's arm, shook his head sternly, and she fell into a sulky silence. "Come now, Coco. Let's get out of their way. I'm sorry." With a forlorn glance towards Pippa, he herded his sister out the door. Finn followed because wherever Colette went, he was sure to go.

Imogene heaved a sigh of relief. "Finally," she said when it was just the four of them. "I thought they'd never leave. I think he would have stayed all afternoon if we'd let him," she said pointedly.

"Oscar's smitten." The comment fell from Rosemary's lips before she could stop it, and she studied Pippa's face for a reaction. Pippa didn't gasp or blush—Oscar's infatuation certainly wasn't news to her—but her lip twitched into something resembling a smile for a split second. Rosemary took it as an encouraging sign and added, "It's kind of sweet, actually, and he's not so bad, is he?"

Pippa didn't have a chance to answer before Imogene scoffed, "He can be smitten all he wants; Pippa is a professional. She knows no good ever comes from becoming romantically entangled with a client."

Rosemary didn't bother to respond even though she

would have liked to. The last thing she wanted to do was continue the argument from the previous evening. She was almost grateful for the work and had lost track of time when a loud bang followed by a spate of exclamations interrupted the conversation. She followed her friends and the noise along the corridor, up the staircase, and into the library. This time, it wasn't the scream of a dying woman, and there was no dead body on the carpet, much to Rosemary's relief.

Mrs. Doon poked her head out of a piece of displaced paneling on the left side of the rear portion of the fireplace. "I've found it!" She clapped her hands and fairly danced with eager excitement.

Footsteps sounded on the stairs, pounding closer as Finn raced into the room, followed by Oscar. "Is anyone hurt? Colette?" Fear etched Finn's features, then smoothed out when his fiancée walked in behind him.

"Found what?" Oscar strode over to Mrs. Doon and then ducked into what Rosemary now realized was a secret room behind the fireplace. Everyone else crowded around, and Desmond let out a whistle of appreciation.

"It's like a little private speakeasy," he said, his eyes sparkling for an entirely different reason than Mrs. Doon's had been. It was only a roughly five-by-ten-foot space, but one any liquor enthusiast would quite enjoy. Bottles lined the shelves along the walls, along with crystal goblets and glasses in varying sizes. In the middle squatted two comfortable-looking leather armchairs and a coffee table laden with a large dress box.

Mrs. Russel arrived belatedly, having taken longer than everyone else to reach the library and, wheezing slightly, pressed into the hidden room. When she saw the box, her eyes widened and she breathed, "The Lanvin! Thank the heavens! It hasn't been damaged, has it?"

Pippa helped Mrs. Russel open the box and lift out the gown. All Rosemary saw was a swath of Lanvin blue silk before Colette materialized out of thin air and snatched the dress away from Pippa.

"Ouch!" Pippa exclaimed, taking a step away from Colette and holding her forearm. "What did you do to me?" She pulled her hand back to reveal a trickle of blood oozing from a small, familiar-looking puncture wound.

Gently and with great reverence, Mrs. Russel tugged the garment away from Colette. Unerringly, her fingers hit upon a straight pin of the type used in dressmaking—the tip stained the rust color of dried blood with just the barest hint of bright red at the sharpened end. Pippa's blood.

"You'd better not have left a stain on that silk." Colette glared at Pippa as if she'd pricked herself intentionally.

Rosemary wasn't worried about bloodstains, and she wasn't the only one to gape. The mark on Pippa's arm looked remarkably like the mark on Ruby's neck. She said as much, then regretted speaking out loud.

"If she wasn't injected, the poison must have been administered some other way. It could have been via something she ate or drank. Any evidence would be gone by now, unfortunately."

Chaos erupted, everyone spitting theories, their voices rising to the ceiling and reverberating back to echo even louder until reaching a crescendo that silenced abruptly when a whistle cut through the din.

"What in the hell is going on?" Mr. Pennington boomed from the doorway. "Well? What are you doing in my private space?" he demanded when nobody answered. Leo had come up behind him and now took in the scene with an expression of disapproval.

"Mother's Lanvin has been found," Colette said, "right where Ruby left it."

Mr. Pennington flinched at hearing Ruby's name before his gaze flicked between the dress box and his daughter. He sounded exhausted when he said, "You can't possibly know for sure she's the one who put it here."

Colette grabbed Pippa's arm and yanked it up to show her father. "Ouch!" Pippa complained again and again Colette ignored her.

"Yes, actually, I can. The dress wasn't in here when we searched the library. And look at this mark. It's the same size and shape as the one on Ruby's neck; there's no doubt about it. That and the dried blood on the pin proves she took the gown, and since she denied ever having laid a hand on it, she must have lied."

Surely, if the girl had any sense at all, Rosemary thought, she'd be less concerned about the damnable dress and more worried that everything they'd believed about the murder could now be called into question. If Ruby's puncture wound was inflicted by the dressmaking pin rather than a syringe needle, it meant the poison had been administered another way—most likely even at another time—blowing all of the evidence and theories thoroughly out of the water.

"Colette, I'm warning you," Mr. Pennington said, stalking back into the library and indicating the rest of them ought to do the same. "I've had just about enough of your baseless accusations. You got what you wanted. She's gone, but that doesn't mean you can sully Ruby's good name."

"As if you hadn't done that already. Mother would be disgusted at the thought of that guttersnipe rifling through her prized possessions." Colette drew herself up to her full height. "Believe what you need to believe," she spat. "I know the truth. Ruby stole the gown and stashed it somewhere, never expecting us to launch a house-wide search. She distracted you, waited until we had already searched the library, and moved the dress, intending to return later and fetch it. Which she would have done if she hadn't died here."

In his role as peacemaker, Oscar put himself between his father and his sister before things got even further out of hand. "We're all a bit overwrought just now. Let's not say things we might regret later. Mother liked her possessions well enough but wouldn't have wanted her family to become fractured over a silly bit of cloth and a few buttons."

Had Vera been there, Rosemary thought, poor Oscar might have been forced to eat those words.

"Oscar's right." Mrs. Doon came forward to put her hand on his arm affectionately. "We should all listen to him."

"It's more than a dress to me," Colette flared, her face showing more anguish than anger. "Father will never understand. He's incapable of more than the base level of human decency."

Oscar watched the emotions cross his father's face and opened his mouth as if to speak but, unable to find the words, snapped it shut.

"You're just like your mother, putting wealth before people." Mr. Pennington pointed to the dress and then to Colette, his eyes flashing with rage, and then he delivered the knockout punch. "You're going to end up bitter, with nothing but your grudges to keep you company, just like she did."

Chapter Fifteen

Colette's face fell, but before it hardened to stone, she looked again like the sad girl Rosemary sometimes saw inside. "You're a monster," she spat at her father bitterly, "I already figured that out, but now everyone can see it."

"All right, let's just calm down." Leo stepped in and reiterated Oscar's attempt to defuse the moment. "Why don't you let me help you back to bed, Mr. Pennington." He spoke in a soothing voice that only served to aggravate Colette further.

"Oh, just stop, you sycophantic little leech," she said, turning her ire in his direction. "Who do you think you are to talk to him like that? He's not a child, and you're not his keeper. You're his *man of all work*, but it's not meant to be taken quite as literally as you do."

Leo said through clenched teeth, "You ought to be ashamed of yourself for acting like a shrew. Don't you possess even a shred of decency?"

"That's rich, coming from you," Colette fired back. "I know all about how Ruby used to undress in front of the upper windows while you were in the courtyard clipping away at the topiaries. Maybe you're the one who killed her—to keep her quiet and keep your job."

Mr. Pennington's head snapped up, and his eyes landed on his daughter. "What are you talking about?" he demanded through clenched teeth.

"I think my explanation fairly well sums it up, don't you? What more do you need to know?" she replied miserably. Rosemary could see that Colette was in pain, but that was no excuse for her current behavior.

Sniffing her distaste, Mrs. Doon muttered something about Leo not being the only man in the house to fall under Ruby's spell.

"It's not...that's not what happened." Leo tried to defend himself, but Mr. Pennington interrupted before he could continue.

"I've heard enough. If anyone else would like to disparage my dead fiancée, please jot down your insults and save them for a later date."

"Can I be of any further service?" Leo asked miserably.

"You're dismissed for the day." Mr. Pennington waved him off, refusing to meet his gaze, and said, "I'll be in my room, and I'd prefer not to be disturbed by anyone," before stalking out of the library.

When he was gone, Leo turned to Colette as if prepared to drop another insult but seemed to think better of it. Instead, he took Mr. Pennington's lead and stormed out without a word.

Oscar turned on his sister then. "You have to stop, Coco. I know Father hurt your feelings, but your actions make the whole family look bad. The tabloids are having a field day; we're fighting in front of our guests and the staff. It's embarrassing, and if you keep this up, you'll put the family's—and the business's—reputation at stake. Not to mention, our mother would be mortified if she saw you acting like this! Haven't you done enough damage already?"

"Take his side; you always have, unless you were taking Mother's. Whichever was the opposite side from me, wasn't that it? Maybe Father's illegitimate child would have been a better sibling than you are," she blurted, her fists at her side and her chest heaving with anger.

Oscar inhaled sharply, and all the color drained from his face. The man was visibly shaken; if Colette's revelation wasn't news to him, Rosemary felt certain he'd missed his calling and ought to follow Vera onto the stage.

Mrs. Doon broke the heavy silence. "How could you devastate your brother that way? What a horrible accusation to make about your father!"

"It's not an accusation if it's true." Colette's face was horribly pale, and her hands turned to fists at her side. "And it is. I read it in Mother's diary."

Mrs. Doon's eyebrows shot to her hairline.

"No." Oscar's voice sounded rough as he forced it between clenched teeth. "It can't be true. You're lying."

Colette's mouth opened and closed a couple of times, and her eyes were filled with pain and regret when they landed on her brother. His, however, had hardened to stone. Suddenly, Oscar Pennington looked more like his father than ever before—shrewd, calculating, and, to top it off, dangerous.

"This is too much." Finn turned away from Colette and, for the first time, regarded her with something other than adoration.

"What does it say when even your humble lapdog thinks you've gone too far? I guess Finn's patience does have a limit, after all. Be careful, sister, or Father will be right—you'll end up a sad, sorry old maid with nothing but your bulging purse to keep you company." Oscar stalked out, in a way not unlike his father and Leo had done minutes earlier.

After a pause, Finn also followed suit. Left behind, Colette watched them go. She said not a word but closed her eyes and took several deep breaths before simply walking out herself.

"Well I never!" Mrs. Russel exclaimed once the

awkward atmosphere had dissipated slightly.

"That girl has been a trial ever since she was in the womb." Mrs. Doon spit venom. "She should have been shipped off to boarding school when she was a child and taught to be a lady."

Once again, Rosemary felt conflicted. Colette was hurting, but she wasn't a child who hadn't yet learned decorum, and her behavior certainly was unbecoming. Yet, Mrs. Doon overlooked the fact that if Mr. Pennington knew his daughter at all, he ought to have known his vicious comment would devastate her. Rosemary felt a rush of pride in the knowledge that her family would never treat one another the way the Penningtons did.

The smug feeling only lasted a moment before she was distracted by Imogene addressing Mrs. Doon. "I suppose you'd rather she suffer in silence than kick up a fuss. As long as things *look* nice and tidy, they must *be* nice and tidy." Rosemary wondered ruefully if Imogene realized she was actually sticking up for the girl she'd sworn to despise.

"Nothing is tidy in this house," Mrs. Russel said, attempting to defuse the tension.

"Well, how could it be with Mr. Pennington gallivanting about while his wife attempted to maintain some semblance of a decent reputation?" Imogene wanted to know. "Is anyone truly shocked that there's an illegitimate child out there? The real surprise would be if there's only one."

Desmond stroked his chin. "What do you suppose happened to the child?"

Somehow, the thought had yet to occur to anyone else, but Imogene quickly devised a theory. "Perhaps it didn't survive. That could have been what Jade referred to in her diary. She said she ought to feel sorry but that someone was getting what she deserved. Perhaps she considered it poetic justice." The idea didn't seem to make Imogene feel any better about the passage. Her eyebrows remained knit together, and she swallowed hard.

Mrs. Russel shook her head disapprovingly. "We shouldn't be discussing the Pennington family's affairs."

On that, and perhaps only that, she and Mrs. Doon shared an opinion.

Chapter Sixteen

Although she wouldn't care to admit it, Vera had considered her film audition a mere formality, given it had been her mother who set the whole thing up. However, her visions of champagne and caviar had been dashed, and there was only one person she was willing to confide in.

"It was an utter disaster," she explained to Rosemary while they readied themselves for dinner. "A cattle call, with a roomful of girls who would do anything to be cast in the role. Positively humiliating."

"And yet you were called back for tomorrow. How bad could it have been?"

"Bad, Rosie. Really bad. That's why I've insisted on seeing this film tonight. It's the studio's latest production, and if it's terrible, I'm simply not going to that audition."

It sounded to Rosemary like Vera rather hoped it would be terrible, but knowing Vera as well as she did, she kept that thought to herself.

"Should we have invited Imogene?" It was an innocent enough question, given Rosemary had yet to fill Vera in on the state of things.

"What do you think of her?"

Vera shrugged. "She seems nice enough. A little territorial, maybe, but she knows what she wants and isn't afraid to go after it."

"Desmond, you mean."

Another shrug from Vera. "I think you've got it the wrong way around because he's the one doing the chasing."

"That's true. There's just something about her that puts my hackles up, and I, for one, would be happy to have a night out where it's just us. It feels like we've been picked up by a whirlwind these past few days."

"That sounds perfect to me." Vera smiled. "I'd rather depend on the opinions of my closest friends when it comes to this movie business anyway. And while Tuesday is an inventive soul, her cocktails pack a punch. I'd rather not have a foul head in the morning."

Desmond grumbled a bit during the cab ride and cast a look at Rosemary that said he thought she was the reason Imogene hadn't been invited. Still, he kept his opinion to himself and, as the others also did, thoroughly enjoyed the film.

"You have to go to that audition," he told Vera on the

way out of the cinema.

With her hand tucked into the crook of Freddie's arm, Vera looked back at the marquee, then responded. "I think you're right. It's worth the trouble to be part of something good."

"Quite so, my darling." Freddie lifted his arm and whistled as a taxi slid around the corner heading in their direction. "The Roosevelt," he ordered once everyone was settled and the driver asked where they needed to go.

"How do you lot feel about a drink? I, for one, could use a stiff whiskey after that," Desmond said hopefully.

Rosemary failed to suppress a sigh and, when she looked back on the evening later, admitted she might have also rolled her eyes—just a little bit. Unfortunately, neither escaped Desmond's notice, and his expression turned stormy. He'd been patient, but now he'd had enough.

"Why are you acting this way, Rose? In all the years we've known each other, I can count on one hand the number of times I've heard you refuse a drink. Under normal circumstances, you'd have to be on your deathbed to let a G&T go to waste, so what is it?"

"Nothing, Des. Nothing at all," Rosemary replied, determined to keep her thoughts to herself.

Unfortunately, Desmond wasn't about to take *nothing* for an answer. "You've been a pill for days. This is supposed to be an enjoyable holiday, and you're ruining it!"

"*I'm* ruining your holiday? What about the dead body in the library? A library I wouldn't have been in at all if it hadn't been for *your* friend."

"Oh, so that's what it is? This is about Imogene, then," Desmond scoffed. "I should have known. It isn't Imogene's fault someone got rid of Ruby Snow. And do you know, it's just occurred to me that one could, if they were paying attention, think *you* are the unlucky charm? If your record stands, you could have stumbled upon a dead body at the zoo, or at Yankee Stadium, or maybe in the lobby of our bloody hotel! It wouldn't be the first time."

The cab driver glanced curiously in the rearview mirror.

"Oh, so I'm a bringer of death. Is that what you're saying?"

"Not a bringer, but a harbinger, it seems! We were destined to become embroiled in yet another investigation, so why not at the Pennington mansion? It's practically a museum, after all. Isn't that exactly where you want to be, amongst the stuffy two-hundred-year-old art?"

"That's a bit harsh, old chap." Frederick might have been talking to the wind for all the notice Rosemary and Desmond took of him.

"You're just looking for a row because you can't stand that I don't think the sun rises and sets on Imogene the way you do," Rosemary retorted.

"What's not to like? What exactly has she done to you, Rose, aside from trying to be your friend? Is it because she's just as intelligent as you are? That's it, isn't it? You simply can't stand that there's another woman around who might be capable of solving a murder!"

"Hey!" Vera protested, turning from her position in the front of the cab and glaring at Desmond. "What am I? Some sort of simpleton?"

Desmond shot her a glare that said she'd be better off keeping out of it. Had he been the only one, she might have wound up another retort, but the warning written across Rosemary's face made Vera's mouth snap shut.

"She blinds you, and you're going to end up with a broken heart."

"It's my heart, Rose, and you didn't care this much about it when I offered it to you on a silver platter, did you? Why do you get to decide if she's worthy enough for me to risk it again now?"

Rosemary didn't know exactly how to answer that question, so she replied irritably, "Then why do you care if I don't like her? You enjoy the chase, the challenge, that's all. You're only interested because she's still all shiny and new. As soon as things begin to tarnish, you'll make your exit."

"If it's just a matter of time before I tire of her, why is it any skin off your nose? It has to be one or the other, Rose," Desmond said with a shake of his head. "She'll either destroy me, or I'll tire of her. That's the same risk anyone ever takes in any relationship. Or maybe that's the problem—you can't bring yourself to take a real risk. Is that why you picked Max instead of me? Because he's the safer bet?"

They'd been children the last time Desmond had spoken to Rosemary so harshly, and even then, it was only because she'd cantered off on one of the horses and left him and Frederick searching for her for over an hour. It stung, but they weren't children anymore, and if Rosemary remembered correctly, she'd ridden away that day because her brother and Desmond had refused to take her down to the brook like they'd promised to do.

"Leave Max out of this, Des. I'm warning you."

"Oh, you're warning me, are you? Why, Rose, because you can't stand to hear the truth?"

Rosemary wasn't certain how things had gotten so far out of hand, but she felt helpless to stop the words from falling out of her mouth. "We can't all follow along behind you on another of your misguided quests for the affections of yet another woman who doesn't fancy you." When they registered for Desmond, his cheeks turned ruddier than beetroot.

The cabbie's eyes flicked back and forth between the mirror and the road, and he'd stopped bothering to pretend he wasn't listening avidly. At any other time, Rosemary would be appalled at her own behavior. Arguing in front of a perfect stranger wasn't her way.

"You're wrong, you know, and so was I," Desmond said, his voice acid. "The problem isn't that you don't think the sun rises and sets on Imogene—it's that she doesn't, like everyone else in your life, think *you* hung the moon. She doesn't see you as perfect Rosemary who can do no wrong, and you simply can't stand it."

Her knee-jerk reaction was to balk. "I couldn't care less how I'm perceived; I only care how I look for the sake of my family, and you know it!"

Desmond balked. "Pfft. You've always cared far more about your image than you let on. You've just been too vain to admit it aloud."

"Vain?" Rosemary quailed when she heard herself speak. Drat the man for making her sound just like her mother. "It's good to know what you do think of me, Desmond."

With that, Rosemary clamped her mouth closed and refused to so much as glance in his direction. He returned her sanctimonious silence, and neither said another word until long after the cab had delivered them back to the hotel.

"He's infatuated with her, and I'm worried about him

170

because I can see she doesn't feel the same," Rosemary said later to Vera, pacing across the carpeted floor of the hotel sitting room until the fibers crackled beneath her toes with static electricity.

Vera sat on the settee, an unlit cigarette in her hand, and watched her friend with a raised eyebrow. "She's not the devil, Rosie. I think she just wants to be friends."

"That's not what Desmond wants," Rosemary insisted, "and we both know how fragile his heart can be."

"I hate to have to be the voice of reason, truly. In fact, I resent you for forcing me into the role, but honestly, Rosie, Desmond is a big boy, and he can handle himself. He's invested, and I don't want to see him hurt any more than you do, but you know you've forgotten something, don't you?" Vera paused for dramatic effect. "She's not the only one who can hurt him, and you seem to be doing a fine job of it."

Chapter Seventeen

Thursday dawned bright and sunny, and Rosemary wished more than anything she could spend the morning wandering around Central Park—in appropriate shoes, of course. She'd apologized Desmond, who was determined to follow Imogene back to the Pennington mansion, and since Frederick and Vera were both otherwise occupied with work—acting responsibly, no less!—she couldn't think of an excuse not to join him.

Kicking up a fuss and convincing him not to go would only have angered Desmond more. They likely would have spent the day in awkward silence even if he'd agreed. Better to let him pair off with Imogene while Rosemary helped Mrs. Russel with the final wardrobe preparations, keeping her eyes open, as promised, for anything Vera might wish to bid on. She suspected that with the auction slated for the following day, Mrs. Russel could use all the help she could get.

"Break a leg," Rosemary said cheerfully before Vera

left for her callback audition, wishing she could instead beg her to skip the whole thing. Spending the day uptown would be infinitely more enjoyable with her best friend by her side, acting as a buffer.

The cab ride was mercifully swift, at least, and when they got there, Rosemary was pulled away almost immediately. "Thank goodness you're here," Pippa gushed when they'd been ushered in through the front door by a sour-faced Mrs. Doon. "I'm in desperate need of your art expertise. Would you mind terribly?"

Without waiting for an answer, Pippa linked arms with Rosemary and pulled her away, telling Imogene over her shoulder, "We'll meet you in the library when we're through."

Half an hour later, Mr. Pennington wandered into the library, a crystal glass filled with whisky in each hand.

"Well, hellooo, ladies," he said, wiggling his eyebrows and slurring. "And gentleman." He nodded to Desmond almost as an afterthought, his head bobbing for a long moment. The motion continued down his body, forcing him to sink onto the settee in front of the fireplace with an audible sigh.

Mr. Pennington's eyes landed on the rug where Ruby had met her end only a few days before, and he seemed to sober slightly—enough to notice both his hands were full. He knocked back one of the whiskies and set the glass on top of the impossibly expensive-looking antique coffee table, leaving a wet streak that would turn into a white ring if left to sit. Rosemary itched to wipe it clean. "Have a drink with me," Mr. Pennington implored, directing the comment at Desmond. "I'll even break out the good stuff."

"Well, I've got work to do," Imogene said quickly, grabbing Pippa and making a speedy escape with an only a half-apologetic backward glance.

Desmond's jaw clenched, and his eyes locked with Rosemary's for a brief moment, but then he looked away and took a seat.

When he'd collected his bearings, Mr. Pennington lumbered to his feet and disappeared inside the secret room behind the fireplace. He returned with an ornate bottle filled with clear liquid along with a couple of glasses. "A prospective business associate sent me a bottle of the best agave tequila money can buy."

"Quite a gift," Desmond said perfunctorily.

Mr. Pennington smiled a bleary smile. "Just one of the perks of sitting at the head of the table," he said, popping the cork off the bottle. "You won't find anything more authentic; I promise you that." He took a long sniff of the contents and then passed the bottle to Desmond, indicating he should do the same. When Desmond's eyes began to water, Rosemary considered making some excuse to join Pippa and Imogene.

With no remorse, Desmond passed her the bottle and

raised an eyebrow in challenge. Rosemary took a delicate sniff and shivered with disgust. The thought of swallowing the stuff made her stomach roll over on itself. "No, thank you," she said, not caring whether Mr. Pennington thought she was impolite.

"Not a risk taker, I see," Mr. Pennington said, nodding sagely. When Desmond smiled smugly, Rosemary wanted to retort that he oughtn't to put so much stock in the musings of a drunk imbecile but managed to hold her tongue.

Mr. Pennington poured two generous glasses, handed one to Desmond, and then resumed his position on the settee, balancing the other on his knee.

"I've made a right mess of things," said Mr. Pennington, clearly at least two cups under and tending towards melancholy. "I had a good woman in Jade, but I didn't appreciate her. Then, I found Ruby, and now, she's gone, too."

He raised his glass. "To Ruby." Feeling forced by circumstance, Desmond took a slug of the strongly scented tequila. It burned all the way down, and his face screwed up into a knot. Rosemary assumed it tasted as bad as it smelled. Considering it smelled like it could strip varnish off the furniture, that was no mean feat.

"I'm swearing off women altogether. They're more trouble then they're worth, and you can't trust them not to go and die on you."

"Or to keep a civil tongue." Desmond aimed the remark at Rosemary, went so far as to raise the glass in a toast to her, and took a second sip of his drink.

The next several minutes passed in silence save Mr. Pennington occasionally mumbling something indistinct. Just when Rosemary thought he might fall off to sleep and release her from enduring his company, he got a second wind.

"Hey, there," Mr. Pennington said, peering at Desmond accusingly, "you haven't finished your glass. Don't you drink tequila?"

Desmond wanted to retort that he did drink tequila, just not usually before ten in the morning, but he knew it wouldn't make any difference, so he took another healthy sip of the offending liquid.

Mr. Pennington let out a roar. "It might be best to take it all in one shot," he said, his eyebrow raised in challenge.

Never one to back down, Desmond raised the glass and made to down it, but then his face turned white as a sheet, and he began to cough.

"We've got a lightweight on our hands," Mr. Pennington slurred with a laugh.

Desmond continued coughing, and the glass fell out of his grasp, dropping onto the coffee table with a crash, a splash, and a tinkle of broken glass. Rosemary's heart filled with fear as he gagged, holding his hands around his throat. Sweat rolled down Desmond's face, and his pupils grew to twice their normal size. With one last choked gasp, he slumped back onto the settee, and that was when Rosemary began to scream.

CHAPTER EIGHTEEN

It only took her a moment to come to her senses, and when she did, Rosemary closed her mouth abruptly and rushed to Desmond's side. "Help me," she demanded from Mr. Pennington, but the man who claimed to have found the cure for half a dozen different illnesses proved himself inept in a medical crisis.

Fortunately, her cries had alerted more of the household, and just then, Imogene burst into the room with Pippa, Oscar, and Mrs. Doon at her heels. Oscar took one look at Desmond and said sternly, "Mrs. Doon, go fetch the eye drops from my night table. Pippa, find Leo and tell him to call the doctor. He needs to get here now, and he needs to bring a dose of pilocarpine."

Imogene had rushed to Desmond's side and she and Rosemary followed Oscar's instructions to help make him more comfortable. When their gazes met, Imogene's eyes filled with emotion—fear, sadness, and regret—but Rosemary held on to her anger like a life raft.

If anything happened to Desmond, it would be Imogene's fault for getting them involved with the Penningtons in the first place, and Rosemary would never forgive her. The moment threatened to draw out, long and awkward, but Oscar volleyed a barrage of questions until Mrs. Doon arrived with the eye drops.

She handed them over, and Oscar ripped open the cap, pouring the vial into the empty glass that had held Mr. Pennington's perfectly benign whisky. "Drink this," he said, holding it up to Desmond's lips.

"What's going to happen to him?" Imogene asked Oscar, her voice almost a whisper. "Is he going to die?"

"He's lucky it wasn't introduced directly into his bloodstream. I don't think he ingested enough for it to be fatal, and it sounds as though he ate a hearty breakfast, so that's another point in his favor. He needs the antidote, pilocarpine. There's a small amount of it in my eye drops, and it should stabilize him until the doctor arrives."

In truth, it wasn't long before Leo delivered the doctor, though it felt like longer to Rosemary, who was forced to watch the color slowly drain from Desmond's face all the while. While he was being tended to, Oscar took charge of making arrangements, glancing every so often at Mr. Pennington, who sat in the corner, watching helplessly.

179

By then, the entire household had gathered to gawk from the entrance of the library, Colette clinging to Finn like a barnacle on a boat.

"He can't be moved, I'm afraid, under any circumstances," the doctor explained once the antidote had been administered and Desmond rested quietly. "He needs to rest. Let the poison work its way out of his system."

Oscar waved a hand. "I've already tasked Mrs. Doon with setting up one of the guest bedrooms for Mr. Cooper. Of course, he's welcome to stay until he makes a full recovery."

"Very well. I'll send a nurse along, if it pleases," the doctor added helpfully, then allowed Mrs. Doon to show him out, reciting instructions all the way.

"I'm not leaving him," Rosemary said once he'd gone. "And neither will my friends when they arrive." She planted herself firmly in Oscar's path, but it turned out there was little need.

Before he could answer, Mr. Pennington spoke from the corner where he was still ensconced. "You'll all be our guests, of course." It sounded as though he was inviting them all for a lovely holiday.

"He didn't drink any of that, did he?" Oscar asked, eyeing his father with some concern. "He doesn't look so great."

"No, he didn't drink any of the tequila, but he's at

least six fingers into the whisky, maybe more."

Oscar appeared embarrassed, even more so when his gaze flicked to Pippa, who had been loitering near the edge of the room, nervously pacing a path in the carpet. "Take my father to his room, won't you?" he implored Leo.

Instead of jumping to service, as he normally would have, Leo glanced at Mr. Pennington nervously.

"He doesn't want your help, does he?" Colette snapped before her father could answer for himself. "I don't know why you haven't been sacked yet."

"Run along, Coco. You're not helping anyone, either." Oscar looked right through his sister. It was his attitude more than the situation that made her obey.

"Fine. Come along, Father. You need some quiet time." Casting one more wistful glance at Oscar, Colette tugged on Mr. Pennington's arm.

He rose with some difficulty, turned towards Desmond as if there was something he wanted to say, then his face went blank, and he let Colette lead him from the room with Leo trailing behind.

By the time Frederick and Vera arrived, Desmond had been tucked into a plush bed in one of the guest rooms, and though he wasn't alert enough to speak, his breathing was steady and his color less deathly pale than it had been before.

Frederick came through the door wearing a look of

wild panic. "What happened," he demanded, noting and ignoring the tension between his sister and Imogene, who flanked Desmond's bed in awkward silence.

"He was poisoned." Rosemary stated the obvious and received an exasperated glare from her brother in response. It was enough to bring her to her senses, and she proceeded to tell the whole story, in detail, while her brother, Vera, and Imogene listened intently. "Mr. Pennington said he was sent that tequila by a prospective business associate, but I don't think any of us believe for a moment that this was an outside job."

Imogene balked. "The difficult part of the story to believe is that the man poured himself a drink and then didn't actually take a sip. If any of you are buying that, I've got some waterfront property in the Sahara to sell you."

"Are you suggesting that Mr. Pennington spiked his own tequila?"

"It would be a brilliant ruse, wouldn't it?"

"See," piped up Frederick, "I told you Mr. Pennington was the murderer!"

"You've got it all wrong, you know." Leo stepped into the room from the corridor and startled Vera, whose back was to the door, half out of her seat.

"Make a noise, wouldn't you?" she snapped. "It's impolite to sneak up on people."

"It's also impolite to eavesdrop," Frederick said.

"How long have you been standing out there?"

Leo scoffed. "I wasn't holding a glass to my ear; I was coming down the stairs and overheard. And what I'm doing isn't nearly as impolite as accusing your host of murder. Mr. Pennington was besotted with Ruby. He never would have done anything to hurt her."

It seemed all of Imogene's give-a-care had evaporated because she snapped, "You can put him on a pedestal all you like, but Mr. Pennington did plenty to harm his wife, so why should we believe him incapable of this?"

"Everyone in this house is capable of murdering Ruby and poisoning your friend," Leo retorted. "I was here earlier today when Mr. Pennington received that bottle of tequila, and I can assure you it was a surprise. Furthermore, he's the only one who fancies the stuff, so who else would it have been meant for?"

Having sniffed the tequila herself, Rosemary thought it was no wonder the rest of the household chose to abstain.

When Leo spoke again, his words echoed the conclusion Rosemary was in the process of making.

"The way it looks to me is that Mr. Pennington was the intended victim all along, and he could still be in danger. You should really be worrying about whether the killer is going to strike again—not following wild theories about my employer."

Leo's show of loyalty might have been touching, but

it did nothing to convince Imogene.

"Since you seem to know so much, maybe it was you who poisoned Ruby, or you and Mr. Pennington are working together. We all know Jade was the one with the money. Maybe Ruby was just a bit too greedy, and you both decided she had to go."

Visibly disgusted, Leo refused to rise to the bait and respond out of anger.

"Look, Ruby thought she could have her cake and eat it, too. She tried to get me to," his face reddened, "take her to bed. When I said no, she threatened to tell Mr. Pennington that I was the one who made advances, and she rebuffed me. I refused to pay her a penny and told her she could have me fired if she wanted to, and she backed down. I have no idea who killed her, but I'd be willing to shake his or her hand and consider it a favor well done. Mr. Pennington could do a lot better than a woman like Ruby."

"That will be quite enough." No one had heard Mr. Pennington come back downstairs and take up a post just outside the door to listen in on the conversation. Apparently, Leo wasn't the only eavesdropper in the house. "Miss Quinn, consider yourself dismissed for the day. You may leave, and take Miss Langley, and Leo with you. I will not tolerate such disrespect in my own home."

"My pleasure," Imogene said, and stalked from the

room.

Stunned by the turn of events, Pippa burst out, "But the auction!"

"I don't give a damn about the damnable auction. I want you out of my house. Now!"

"Pippa, wait." Oscar glared at his father as he followed Pippa from the room. "I'm sorry, he doesn't mean it."

"Leave me be, Oscar." Pippa's voice wafted back as she moved purposefully down the stairs.

Chapter Nineteen

"I need to get out of here," Rosemary said, smoothing the front of her dress for what felt like the hundredth time. She couldn't stand sitting there, staring at Desmond any longer. He looked so frail and helpless, and she couldn't stop replaying in her head the last angry words they'd exchanged. Their row hung over his sick bed like a pall nearly as bad as death. "I need some air. I'll take a cab back to the hotel and pack up some of his things."

"Why don't you go with her, darling," Frederick said to his wife, "and arrange for our bags to be delivered here. I'm not leaving his side, so it looks as though we'll be staying until he's strong enough to be moved." He puffed out his chest. "Anyone wishing him further harm will have to get through me first."

Vera kissed Frederick squarely on the lips before taking leave. "I pity any fool who underestimates your devotion."

Outside, Rosemary lit a rare cigarette and took a long drag. After a few puffs, the cab arrived, and she flung it into the street. Full of bluster, she clambered into the backseat and huffed out their destination, Vera's eyes on her the entire time.

"This is all Imogene's fault. We wouldn't have even been here if she hadn't been so intent on stringing Desmond along to get him to be her beast of burden," Rosemary ranted once the cab pulled away from the curb. "He's positively enamored of her, and she's playing him for a fool!"

Vera raised an eyebrow at the statement but didn't engage.

"She's an opportunist." Rosemary continued raving. "She might as well have poisoned him herself. Perhaps she did!"

Vera's mouth turned down as she frowned, and she couldn't keep quiet anymore. "You think Imogene spiked Mr. Pennington's tequila in order to poison Desmond? Even if she could engineer such a thing, why would she? They're friends, and you said she's already turned down his offer of a loan, didn't you? What else could she want?"

That—Vera's excellent and not at all insane point—caused Rosemary a fleeting moment of pause, but just as anyone with a vehement wish to avoid the truth would, she thought up a reason quite quickly and retorted, "Perhaps she's after more than just a loan. Desmond's got scads more money, hasn't he?"

"If she was dastardly enough to want to steal all his money, wouldn't she reel him in with her feminine wiles, marry him, and *then* bump him off? She would hardly benefit by poisoning him now. Can you hear yourself? I've never seen you like this, Rosie," Vera pointed out, "so consumed with rage. I think you might have finally gone off your rocker. You do realize you sound like an absolute raving lunatic?"

But Rosemary didn't realize it, at least not then. She would later, with horror, but for now, she only retorted indignantly, "Why is it that when you think your understudy is out to get you, I'm expected to hate her, no questions asked, but now that I have a problem with Imogene, you can't simply back me up?"

"I don't know," Vera replied testily, "perhaps for the same reason why when I wanted to put burrs in Frederick's sweaters, you stopped me. And we aren't children anymore. We're adults now, Rosie, even Frederick. You sound just like he used to sound, callous and unsympathetic, always jumping to conclusions."

"You married him," Rosemary mumbled in reply.

Vera sighed. "I married him because he grew up. I wouldn't have been proud to call him my husband back then, and quite frankly, I'm feeling similarly about you right at this very moment. Are you going to have a row with me now, as well? Perhaps later, you could scold your brother or make a small child cry."

Before Rosemary could respond, the cab came to a stop. "Here you are," the driver said, but Vera didn't move to get out. When Rosemary looked out her window, she realized why. Instead of the façade of The Roosevelt Hotel, Rosemary realized she was looking at the front of the Red Door.

"What? When did you change our destination?" she demanded.

With a sigh and a roll of her eyes, Vera turned to face her dearest friend. "Rosie, darling, you gave him this address when he picked us up in front of the Pennington mansion. Obviously, your subconscious is telling you that you need to work this out with Imogene. Now, why don't you go inside, and I'll return to the hotel and round up our things. Go on," she said, making a shooing motion with her hands when Rosemary appeared unwilling to budge. "I won't take no for an answer."

Rosemary knew that while she could talk Vera into doing just about anything, the same applied in reverse; she wouldn't refuse her friend a thing, particularly not when Vera was right, and she'd been an absolute pill. The tension between her and Imogene had become more than merely palpable, and one way or another, their quarrel needed to be put to rest—for Desmond's sake, if nothing else.

The bell on the door tinkled cheerfully, in stark contrast with her mood when she entered the Red Door antiquities shop. She took a few steps forward at a clip until Imogene looked up disapprovingly from where she bent over a table laid with a tea set unlike any Rosemary had ever seen before.

"I need to talk to you."

Imogene adjusted the eyeglasses perched on the end of her nose. "We can talk, but only if you take a deep breath and agree to do it calmly. I can't have anything upsetting these teacups, and quite frankly, this is my place of business, and I refuse to sully it. Either calm down and take a seat or leave."

That hadn't been what Rosemary was expecting from the self-proclaimed hothead. "How can you sit here and tell me to calm down when Desmond is on his deathbed at the Pennington mansion?" She was angry and had expected the same from Imogene. Expected, if she was being honest, to engage in a knock-down, drag-out argument that would somehow release all her anger and make her feel better.

"He's not going to die," Imogene said sharply. "He can't. And you shouldn't put that sort of energy out into the universe."

The comment caught Rosemary off guard. She plopped into the chair across from Imogene and watched with curiosity as Imogene methodically poured water from a kettle into each of the ancient-looking teacups. "What are you doing?"

"I'm awakening and resetting an antique Yixing unglazed tea service."

Despite herself, Rosemary had to ask. "Awakening?"

"These pieces are close to two hundred years old, and if they aren't properly cared for, they'll crack and crumble. I've had to soak and simmer the teapot several times already." Imogene handed one of the cups to Rosemary, who turned it over in her hands, feeling the weight of it both physically and historically.

"They're a piece of human history. Just think how many people have sipped from these cups. Can you imagine the tales this tea service could tell? Someone has been taking care of it for a very long time. Many someones, throughout the years. I'm just the latest in a line of people—mostly women, I presume—tasked with ensuring it survives."

Moving slowly, Imogene executed a complicated ritual of pouring, swirling, and placing each cup into a precise grouping around the pot, a lovely piece decorated with a raised design of leaves and twigs.

"They weren't so very different from us, either, those women. We like to think we're so advanced, but really, not all that much has changed in the last couple hundred years. We, women, want to have pretty things; to be seen and admired; to display our worth—or our worthiness, as the case may be."

"The burden of being a woman, I suppose. We care, and we take care of the things that matter to us. Take this tea service as an example. It has experienced tenderness and care, even from you, because it matters. The cups in your speakeasy get little to none of your attention. They're a means to an end, and it's the contents that have value, not the cups."

Imogene wrinkled her nose, but Rosemary hadn't meant to insult, and even if she had, there was something to what she'd said.

"I suppose you have a point," Imogene admitted. "The speakeasy itself is no more than a necessity to me. Then you have Jade's collection, which sits on a shelf, always empty, without purpose."

Nodding, Rosemary said, "They're just for show. Like Ruby, I suppose."

A gray tiger cat came streaking out of the back of the shop and hopped up to land abruptly on top of the sideboard that was butted up against one edge of the table where Imogene worked. It went to work cleaning one paw while keeping a suspicious eye on Rosemary.

"Oh, Cat, stop glaring. You aren't in the least bit intimidating." With that, the cat rolled onto its back, feet in the air, and began to purr, a rumble from deep in its belly. Imogene took off her glasses and set them aside, rubbed the cat's stomach for a brief moment, and then fished a flask out of the top of her boot.

She poured a long stream into her teacup and passed it to Rosemary, who did the same before standing up and wandering around the shop as she sipped. It wasn't full of the type of pristine antiques her mother might have fancied, and none of it looked like anything that could be found in the Pennington mansion. Instead, it was all very mysterious and bohemian. A wooden mask hung on the wall to Rosemary's left, its carved features fierce enough to make her shiver.

With no premeditated intention, she blurted, surprising even herself, "It seems like you want to dislike me, despite my best efforts. Why? What have I done? It's been like this since before our row the other night, so that can't be all of it."

"It's not that you did anything," Imogene retorted, stopping mid-sentence abruptly. "Well, that's not entirely true. It's that everything you do is perfect! You command respect, and yet you don't speak out of turn. You never seem to get ruffled, and you can smooth over any situation. Your name is Lillywhite, for heaven's sake—no matter what you do, you come up smelling like roses! It's as though nobody ever doesn't like you!"

"It does usually work that way, but I'd never really noticed before."

Imogene stopped and stared. "Hell, what must that be like?"

"Well, It isn't terrible," Rosemary intoned.

Imogene's eyes widened at the wry comment, and she burst into laughter. Rosemary stared at her for a split second, then joined in. For a few moments, the pair roared, and when they'd quieted down and wiped the tears from their eyes, the tension had finally dissipated.

"You're right," Imogene admitted. "I judged you while assuming you were judging me."

Vera was right; Rosemary had been acting like a raving lunatic. This Imogene didn't seem like she had it out for anyone. She was genuinely worried about Desmond—cared about him, that much was clear.

"I'm not perfect, and I do care how I'm perceived by others. I *want* everyone to like me." Rosemary caught Imogene's gaze. "Just last night, Desmond accused me of the same thing, and I denied it. I lied, both to him and to myself."

Imogene poured another shot from the flask into Rosemary's teacup. "We all care what people think about us. It's not a crime."

"You don't," Rosemary scoffed. "You don't care what anyone thinks of you."

Imogene rolled her eyes. "I've just learned to keep my guard up, is all. If I didn't care, I would have raked every single one of the Penningtons over the coals by now, but on the whole, I keep my opinions to myself. It's not without effort, particularly when it comes to people like Colette. She has everything a young woman could want, and she doesn't appreciate any of it. If she has the sniffles, there's a full staff of doctors and nurses to cater to her every sneeze. Meanwhile, down here, I've got a back-alley quack who makes most of his money helping women out of the family way and sometimes closes bullet wounds. I thought Jade Pennington was my friend, but over the past few days, I've realized we were separated by more than just 59th Street."

"I'm sorry." If Vera had suddenly shown a new, unlikeable side of herself, Rosemary knew she'd be devastated. It didn't seem as if Imogene and Jade had been as close friends, but it still had to hurt.

"I think I'm a shrewd person in business and with people in general, but I never saw the side of Jade that Pippa says she read about in that diary. I knew she wasn't happy in her marriage, and I suppose that could be enough to turn a person sour. She said she didn't want Oscar to turn out like his father."

"Who would?"

Imogene drained the last of her tea. "Oscar might look like his father, and when he wants to, he exhibits the same commanding presence, but he's not a pompous braggart. If Jade visited punishment on Oscar for his father's sins, it wasn't right, and it means she missed out on a connection with her own son."

"If we're going to talk about missed connections,"

Rosemary said, thinking a change of subject might be good and wanting an answer to the burning question. "Why don't you fancy Des? He's a good man. One of the best."

Wrinkling her nose, Imogene took a moment to consider.

"What I've discovered is that I value my independence. I'm set in my ways; that's what I told Desmond, but I don't think he understood. It's not the age difference. It's less than a decade, and lord knows there have been larger gaps than that. It's not even the notion that he might eventually decide he'd prefer a more traditional life with a conventional wife and family. He's handsome, and he has an excellent sense of humor and a wonderful, kind heart. It's...it's..."

"Ineffable," Rosemary finished for her. "Poor Desmond. I hope it's not his fate to continue to be described as such." Suddenly, she sobered. "What if he doesn't have a fate left at all? We have to figure out who's behind these poisonings—for Desmond's sake as well as Mr. Pennington's. He must have been the intended victim, mustn't he?"

Imogene nodded and then, after a long moment, thumped her fist on the desk, jiggling the delicate teacups. "If only the murderer had succeeded. All of this is Mr. Pennington's fault, and now we're back at square one with every suspect on both sides of the house still possessing the means, motive, and opportunity to poison both Ruby and Mr. Pennington."

The shrill sound of the telephone bell interrupted the conversation. Imogene ducked behind the checkout counter and answered, listening for a few long moments before sighing with relief and muttering a quick round of thanks.

"That was Mrs. Doon. Desmond is awake! He's going to be all right."

Rosemary felt her eyes prick with tears, and all the tension and worry and gin seemed to rush to her head. She sank down into the closest chair and took a few deep breaths. "He's going to be all right," she repeated, thinking perhaps she'd only ever been so grateful for a few things in her life, though, at that moment, she couldn't have named a single one.

CHAPTER TWENTY

When Rosemary and Imogene returned to the Pennington mansion, they were ushered in—through the front entrance, no less—by an unusually congenial Mrs. Doon. "Go right on up. Your friend Mrs. Woolridge has just arrived, and I'll be there shortly with Mr. Cooper's tea."

When she'd gone, Imogene said conspiratorially, "It seems all we needed was for our friend to be nearly killed for her to pull the stick out of her rear end and act like a human."

Rosemary let a grin cross her face, but it faded before they reached the guest bedroom where Desmond was ensconced. True to his word, Frederick maintained his bedside vigil while Vera moved about the room, talking a blue streak and fluffing cushions. Desmond watched with heavy lids that popped fully open when Rosemary and Imogene entered, arms linked. Vera cocked one eyebrow and then offered a smug smirk that earned her a rueful eye roll from Rosemary.

"The lengths to which some men will go to garner sympathy of the feminine persuasion," Imogene teased, striding to the bed and giving Desmond a peck on the cheek.

"Worked like a charm," he retorted with a wink.

When his eyes shifted to Rosemary, they softened, and a long look passed between them. "Not to worry, tis merely a flesh wound," he said, defusing any lingering tension.

"Don't let him fool you," warned Vera. "He's stoic—likely thanks to the doctor's potent tonic—but he's going to need a lot of rest and absolutely no agitation."

Desmond's eyes narrowed. "All right, that's enough. Let's talk about something else—anything else. I've already heard what happened at Freddie's meetings—"

"A whole lot of nothing," Frederick interjected irritably.

"—but what about your audition, Vera? How did it go?"

Under normal circumstances, Vera would have given Desmond what for, but she peered at him indulgently and settled into a chair. "I'm afraid you'll be disappointed, Desi, because it was positively awful."

"Now you're being dramatic."

"You do know who you're talking to, don't you?"

Vera laid the back of her hand on her forehead and struck a pose. "Anyway," she continued, "I thought I was meeting with Mr. Allen Senior and the rest of the callback group, but when I arrived, it was just his son—the one Tuesday warned me about. I should have listened. He's a smarmy, self-entitled boob with absolutely no respect for a lady."

The amused smile Frederick had been wearing, assuming his wife was merely razzing Desmond, fell off his face.

"Everything is copacetic, darling," she assured him, smiling when he noticed her use of American slang. "He didn't try anything so blatant as to spur you into action; he kept his hands to himself. I only wish I could say the same for his eyes." Vera made a gagging face. "You know the type. He insinuated that he could help me succeed in the film business—as long as I was willing to do whatever it took to become a star. When I declined—politely, though it took every ounce of self-control I possess—he turned me out. Called me a tease and said I might as well go back to London and content myself with watching from the wings while girls with more *ambition* get top billing."

"Dirty rotten scoundrel."

"What she said." Rosemary nodded her head towards Imogene.

Vera shrugged. "But do you know what bothers me

the most? He's right. Let's face it; if I'm not willing to debase myself, it's unlikely I'll ever be a star."

"Do you really want to be?" Imogene spoke up to inquire. "I had you pegged as a serious actress—more suited to the stage than film. Isn't that where the real actors are?"

"You know, my dear," Frederick said, "you don't have to be famous to be fabulous, no matter what your mother might believe."

Vera opened her mouth to retort but seemed to have second thoughts. Her eyes flicked to Desmond, whose lids had begun to droop, and she busied herself fluffing his pillows. "Come now, Freddie, we've got to let Des get some rest," Vera wheedled, but Frederick refused to budge.

"I'm not leaving him, Vera. There's already one person dead, and someone was trying to make Desmond number two."

"I'll be just fine, mate," Desmond replied, coming back around. "The girls are all here—who would be suicidal enough to try and hurt me with them in attendance? Genie probably has a Derringer in her bootleg."

"Sorry, no boots today." Stepping back, Imogene lifted her leg to show off a pretty pair of heeled pumps.

Desmond swallowed hard, then squinted to remember the thread of the conversation. "And besides, that tequila was obviously meant for Mr. Pennington. I'm quite insulted, in fact, to have been overlooked as a potential victim." Desmond sniffed. "And by the way, it was delivered by courier, so it's possible the dose that killed Ruby also came from outside the house and that nobody here is actually a murderer at all. They may have all been telling the truth about their alibis if you can believe it."

"If that's true and Mr. Pennington was the intended victim in both poisonings, it means the murderer has failed twice. Whoever they are, they're no criminal mastermind. Either that or they have just the worst luck. What were the chances that Mr. Pennington would drink the tequila or that he would drink it alone? Missing the target doesn't appear to have been a concern, so we could be dealing with someone unhinged."

"More unhinged than other kinds of murderers?" Desmond teased, receiving a half-exasperated smirk in reply.

"You joke, but most murders happen in the heat of the moment. Planning it out is another level if you ask me."

Vera shivered. "I suppose it would be easy if one felt justified. When Mr. Cuthburt's murderer had us cornered behind that church, threatening to kill us, all I felt was relief when Max shot him instead. If I'd been able to get hold of the gun, I would have pulled the trigger without hesitation."

"Yes," Rosemary said slowly, "I do believe you would have acted on instinct and slept quite soundly, knowing you'd made the best choice, but only because you were being threatened. If you unwittingly caused harm to an innocent person, your conscience wouldn't give you a moment's peace."

"She's right," Imogene agreed. "Guilt is a normal response, but whoever killed Ruby isn't huddled in a corner, hating themselves; they're trying again."

Vera shivered. "How does one live with a secret like that, do you suppose?"

Frederick was the one who answered. "Probably just like with any other secret," he said. "What choice would a man have, really? He would go about his life acting normally. He meets a friend for dinner, sees a show, shaves his face, and clips his toenails. And at the same time, planning a murder, or at least not counting it out as a possible solution to a problem." At Vera's raised eyebrow, Frederick came out of his reverie and shrugged. "What? It's just a theory."

Imogene began to pace the length of Desmond's bed from head to foot. "What if the murderer had it out for Mr. Pennington and Ruby both?"

"If we knew how Ruby's poison was truly administered, it might give us a clue as to who killed her," Rosemary said. "Oscar and Colette are the most likely to have wanted her out of the picture, but despite the obvious familial strife, I think they both care about their father. It's not out of the question, of course."

Imogene shot her an appreciative nod and admitted, "The same goes for the staff members. I can see most any one of them wanting Ruby out of the house, but they wouldn't need to kill her to make that happen. And if they did, why then proceed to target Mr. Pennington? Surely *he* had no intention of sacking Mrs. Doon or Leo, not that the latter ought to count his job as secure at this juncture. Mrs. Russel retired years ago and is only here as a favor to Jade."

Rosemary looked up at the ceiling and then let out a long sigh. "It might be a stretch, but could there be two murderers? They might have been in on it together, or murderer number two could have been inspired by Ruby's death and decided to bump Mr. Pennington off for an entirely unrelated reason. Either way, Mr. Pennington is still in danger, and so is everyone around him." Desmond glanced at the dinner plate delivered by Mrs. Doon and blanched.

"What about Finn?" Frederick leaned back and crossed his arms.

"Very good, darling." Vera clapped her hands. "You've hit it on the head—only I do think I vaguely recall having said something similar...oh yes! Why, how silly of me. I *did* state right from the beginning that I thought Finn was a suspicious character."

"Yes, dear."

"But why would Finn want to murder Mr. Pennington?" Rosemary asked. "By all counts, Mr. Pennington approves of the match between Finn and Colette. Wouldn't he wait until after they'd married before bumping off his wealthy father-in-law? He has nothing to gain."

"Perhaps Mr. Pennington changed his mind about the match," Imogene suggested. "Colette has money without her father, remember? And if Finn and Ruby *were* having an affair on the side, it would give him motive."

"Maybe we'll get lucky and the killer will try again." Frederick realized he might have put his foot in it. "Not that I'm in favor, mind you. I only mean they've made mistakes so far. One more mistake could give us the answer."

"Like I said, the girls have it under control. Together, they'll figure out who did it in no time flat," Desmond mumbled out of context, having lost track of the conversation again as he began to doze off.

Her voice low, Rosemary said, "He needs his rest, but I feel like I've had three cups of coffee. Vera, did you happen to pack the book that was sitting on my bedside table at the hotel?"

Vera shook her head apologetically. "Sorry, Rosie, but I think you might find something of interest in the library."

Rosemary blanched. "Perhaps I'll simply count sheep until I fall asleep."

"You're not the only one whose love for the library has waned," Frederick commented. "I heard Oscar mention that the idea of tearing this place to the ground was beginning to sound more appealing by the day."

"I have a suggestion," Imogene piped up, "if you're willing to stick your neck out." At Rosemary's raised brow, she elaborated. "I'm here, and I'm wide awake as well; Pippa is probably at home worried sick over how many auction items have yet to be tagged..."

"Sounds like a plan to me," Vera agreed, "but what's that about our necks?"

"Well, I can't imagine Mr. Pennington's patience with me will extend to an overnight visit."

Rosemary opened her mouth, but from his sick bed, Desmond roused one last time, long enough to say, "You leave him to me—or Freddie. *Allez*. En garde," before falling back to sleep.

CHAPTER TWENTY-ONE

In a second unexpected show of kindness, Mrs. Doon even brought in a pot of tea and a plate of biscuits before she retired for the evening, and it turned out Imogene's concerns over being asked to leave the mansion had been unnecessary. Somewhere around one o'clock in the morning, Oscar made his way into the portrait gallery and, to her surprise, insisted on lending a hand. He spent a solid hour lugging some of the heavier items and setting them in place and made even more progress in softening Imogene's opinion of him.

The three women worked through the night, organizing and tagging nearly all of the pieces Pippa had been fretting over. Once they established a system, the work went quickly, leaving plenty of time for conversation. All the theories that had been proposed were thoroughly dissected again, the conclusion being that every suspect had both the means and the opportunity to commit the crime. It all boiled down to motive.

"Have we made too many assumptions on that front? Perhaps it's not as cut and dried as the relationship between Ruby and Mr. Pennington after all. It would help if we knew how she was poisoned and whether the atropine was meant for her or for him all along."

Oscar's warning that due to the nature of poisonings—and atropine in particular—the killer was quite likely to make a clean getaway hung over the trio like a cloud. And it wasn't only Mr. Pennington in danger, as they'd all been forced to learn the hard way.

Finally, just as the sun began rising, Imogene declared, "We're nearly ready. Pippa will be so pleased. You go on now and get some rest." She took Frederick's place at Desmond's bedside, allowing the others a few short hours of sleep.

No sleep might have been better, Rosemary thought when it ironically required three cups of coffee to wake her up the next morning. As a result, she made everyone late to greet Pippa.

Pippa's voice floated into the corridor before they reached the portrait gallery doors. "It's incredible," she breathed. "How? I mean…what? I mean…did you do this?

"I helped a little," came Oscar's reply, "but your friends did the bulk of the work. You're lucky to have people like them in your life."

His voice was filled with sincerity and something perhaps resembling envy. A long moment of silence ensued, and then Pippa reluctantly said, "Well, I still have quite a lot to do before the auction starts."

"See," Rosemary said quietly to Imogene, "she's still focused on her work."

Imogene's head tipped to one side, one strawberry blond curl falling forward to bounce in front of her eyes. She brushed it away thoughtfully. "I don't know; maybe he's not so bad. If he's worthy, he'll let her be who she is. Either way, I suppose it's her decision to make—no matter how it turns out."

"It always is."

Mrs. Doon's head bobbed into view coming up the stairs, cutting off any more discussion on the subject of Pippa's romantic interests.

"Oh, there you all are," Mrs. Doon said. "This place is turning into a zoo. Some of your colleagues from the auction house are here, and Mrs. Russel and I are in need of some assistance with Mrs. Pennington's wardrobe if you wouldn't mind terribly." She approached the portrait gallery door and did a double take when she saw Oscar and Pippa standing so close to one another.

Oscar glanced in the direction of the doorway with a look of disappointment. "Well, I should let you get back to it," he said to Pippa. "The sooner this auction is through, the sooner we can all move on with our lives. I, for one, am looking forward to the next chapter—in my new apartment. I sign the papers next week."

"An apartment?" Mrs. Doon asked, taken aback. "I'd no idea you were planning to move."

"Yes, well, I am," he said shortly. "And you didn't have any idea because, quite frankly, it's none of your nevermind." Oscar stalked past the maid, and her face fell. She turned to go, and when she was gone, Imogene let out a low whistle.

"That was brutal, even if she did deserve it," Pippa said, her warm feelings spilling over to Mrs. Doon. She shook off the thought and turned to Imogene. "Thank you, truly. I spent all last night in a tizzy, searching through the classified ads for job listings—certain I was going to be canned after today, but you saved me!"

"You're welcome. We all worked together. Whatever I've learned about her, I'll not shirk doing my part to honor Jade's final request. I'm looking forward to closing the front door behind me and washing my hands of the Penningtons."

Professional courtesy kept Pippa from voicing a similar sentiment, but Imogene wasn't the only one who would be happy to see the back of the place.

"Let's go give Mrs. Russel that hand." With no sleep at all, Imogene looked fresher than Rosemary felt, which sparked a hint of friendly jealousy.

In Mrs. Pennington's wardrobe, Colette perched on a tufted footstool staring balefully at the nearly empty shelves and racks. She was dressed to the nines once again and didn't deign to assist Mrs. Doon and Mrs. Russel, who bustled around her, sorting the remainder of the garments and accessories into trunks.

"Colette, you'll want the cosmetics, I assume, since you shared your mother's coloring. What about these scarves?" Mrs. Russel held up a fistful of fabric strips. "Are we keeping them, donating them, or throwing them out?" She punctuated the options by holding the scarves over each of the trunks in turn.

"Keeping them."

Mrs. Russel sighed and laid the scarves on top of the trunk already filled to the brim, and Rosemary noted that the other two were empty. She and Imogene set about taking down the items above Mrs. Russel's reach.

"What about these bum rolls?" Vera asked, peering curiously into a hat box she'd pulled from an upper shelf. "They're thoroughly out of fashion these days, but I'll admit to being slightly sad I missed the era of the bustle."

Stepping in front of the oval cheval mirror, Vera tied the bum roll around her waist, then turned to see the full effect.

"That's meant to be worn under your clothes," Mrs. Russel pointed out unnecessarily. "I don't suppose it would fit with that dress you're wearing. These modern fashions make everyone look stick straight." Her disapproval showed in the set of her mouth.

Game to test the theory, Vera loosened the ties slightly to allow for better access and dragged her dress up and over, and it took an effort to yank the material down over the padding. As it turned out, Mrs. Russel was right. Instead of a gracefully plump backside, it looked like Vera was trying to smuggle contraband back there. Lack of sleep sent Rosemary into a fit of giggles, which only intensified when Vera waggled her hips to send the pad dancing.

"Stop. I beg of you." Rosemary could hardly breathe. "Take it off."

However, that was easier said than done, Vera struggled to pull her dress back up and, in the process, managed to spin the bum roll completely around to the front where the empire waist allowed for a better drape.

"Don't let Freddie see you like that. He already wants a family." Rosemary's comment stilled Vera's laughter as thoroughly as if she'd been doused in cold water.

"Help me get this untied." Vera turned her back to Rosemary, who reached up under the frock to pick at the knot. It did not escape Rosemary's notice that Vera cradled the bum roll for a quick moment.

"If you're quite finished," Pippa turned to Vera, "would you mind coming to the ballroom with me? I could use your eye to ensure all the accessories for the wardrobe collection are being properly displayed."

"I'd be delighted." Vera's eyes gleamed at the chance to see if any of the accessories were worth adding to her list of items to bid on. Still holding the bum roll, she shot Colette a questioning glance. "Keep, donate, or throw in the bin?"

"If bin means rubbish, then I have to say bin." Colette eyed the bum roll with distaste. "All of them."

"Some of these were made specially for certain gowns. It might be better to keep them together," Mrs. Russel suggested. "Are you sure you don't want to hold on to them?"

"Didn't I just say I wanted them gone?" Once again, Colette's mood changed with lightning speed.

Mrs. Russel opened her mouth to answer but snapped it shut when Colette growled, "Just leave them. Just leave it all here." She almost looked as though she might cry, but nobody in the room would have been callous enough to point out the fact.

"I'll go help Pippa." Her expression unreadable, Mrs. Russel hurried from the room.

Imogene appraised Colette for a long moment, her eyes raking over the girl's contorted face. "I'm sorry," she said unexpectedly. "This must be very difficult for you."

All her former mirth gone, Rosemary thought Colette

might acknowledge Imogene's kindness, but she only replied with a snotty, "What would you know about it?"

"A lot, actually," came Imogene's reply, her voice even softer than it had been before, to Rosemary's surprise. "You aren't the first girl to lose her mother."

"Well, I'm doing just fine," Colette said, sticking her nose in the air and rising from her seat. "Now, if you'll excuse me, Finn should be here to fetch me any minute. I've no intention of watching the vultures descend—Mother's wishes or not. Father was right about one thing: this auction is unseemly, and we should never have agreed to it. Perhaps if he hadn't been so distracted, he might have put thought into action."

Mrs. Doon let out a harrumph from where she'd all but blended into the wallpaper. "You do know that it takes two to tango, don't you? As abhorrent as that woman might have been, she couldn't have seduced a man who wasn't willing to be seduced—as if such a man exists!"

"Perhaps the faithful ones simply don't fancy old fuddy-duddies like you. My Finn would never be lured in by a trollop like Ruby. He's smarter than that."

"I suppose you would like to think so," Mrs. Doon retorted archly, "but I know the truth. I witnessed the conversation between him and Ruby, and it didn't look innocent to me." Her smug expression indicated she expected Colette to be shocked.

214

Instead, she scoffed. "Witnessed? Didn't look innocent? You didn't actually hear anything specific, did you?" For all her bluster, Colette appeared relieved at the notion. "Whatever reasons Finn had for speaking with Ruby are his own. I trust him, and unless you have proof of something untoward, you can keep your opinions to yourself."

"It wouldn't be the first time I've done so," Mrs. Doon shot back.

Colette's nostrils flared. "You just want to hate me—you always have! You've always favored Oscar and treated me horribly."

"I'm pleasant to your brother because he's pleasant to me. You get what you give, girl, and that's a lesson I pray one day you'll learn. If not for your own sake, for the people who are forced to endure you."

Before Colette could retort, Finn came around the corner whistling a tune. He stopped short when everyone in the room stared at him as though he'd been summoned out of the ether and settled his gaze on Colette questioningly. "Am I late? Or early? Do I have toilet tissue stuck to my shoe?"

Instantly, Colette softened. "Of course not, darling. You're right on time." She tried to smile, but it didn't quite reach her eyes.

"What's going on? Have they been treating you harshly again?" Finn glanced at the assembled group with some accusation.

For some inexplicable reason, Rosemary blurted, "Mrs. Doon claims she saw you and Ruby engaging in a suspicious conversation right before Ruby was poisoned." She received an impressed smirk from Imogene and a death glare from Mrs. Doon.

"What is it, Coco? You can't believe I—"

Colette's eyes were wide, and they flicked away from his for just a moment, long enough to tell Rosemary—and Imogene, unless they'd both tensed at the same time by coincidence—that she wasn't quite as confident as she'd let on. "Of course not, darling," she reassured him.

Finn peered at Colette for a long moment. "Oh, hell. Enough is enough. You want to know the truth?" Colette tensed once more, another infinitesimal movement. "I did know Ruby before she started cavorting with your father."

Mrs. Doon exclaimed triumphantly, "Aha!"

Finn's exasperated expression deepened, but he kept his eyes on Colette. "You see, Ruby used to be a dancer. A dancer of the—ahem—burlesque variety. I saw her about a year ago at an, um, well, at a friend's rather raucous birthday party."

Mrs. Doon's face screwed up into a disgusted sneer, and she spat, "This is the man you want to marry? One who goes gallivanting about town with *burlesque* dancers? So much for him being a stand-up guy."

"Put a lid on it, Mrs. Doon," Colette said, gazing at Finn with rapt attention.

"Ruby tried to blackmail me to keep me from exposing her secret. I told her I didn't intend to tell your father. What would be the point? Either he wouldn't care or, and this is the more likely scenario, he already knew. Mr. Pennington is no dolt, and if Ruby Snow didn't scream *lady of the evening*, I don't know who did. Well, she didn't like that. Didn't believe me. And then she started to get pushy. I suppose I might have let it go too far, but I didn't think it was relevant, and you already hated her so much. I thought it would just fuel your fire and make things even more uncomfortable around here."

"So you lied," Mrs. Doon finished.

"I didn't lie. I kept a fact to myself out of concern for my fiancée, who frankly has been through enough. There's no crime in that."

"No, not in lying alone—but it depends on what else you're lying about, doesn't it?" She leveled him with a steely gaze, one full of suspicion and disgust.

"You think I killed Ruby, don't you, Mrs. Doon?" he asked, his eyes wide and wild. "Suppose I had; wouldn't that then be a dangerous accusation to make?"

Colette's mouth dropped open in shock. "Finn!"

"What?" he asked. "I was only joking." When Colette's look of consternation lingered, he crossed his arms and regarded her through slitted lids. "What is it, Coco? You don't believe I killed her, do you?"

"Well, didn't you?"

Finn's jaw fell towards the floor, Mrs. Doon was rendered entirely speechless, and Rosemary could see Imogene grinning like a lunatic in the corner. "No!" he cried. "Why would you think that I did?"

Now, Colette's cheeks turned a deep shade of crimson. "Well, I thought perhaps it meant—well, that you might have done it for me. I thought it might have meant that this was more than just a marriage of convenience like what my mother and father had." When Finn remained silent, her voice turned into a pout. "People have done stranger things for love, you know."

Mrs. Doon had built up a full head of steam during the last bit of the conversation. "You must be joking—or mad! You're disappointed that he didn't commit murder just to please you?"

For a long moment, Finn stood staring—everyone, truth be told, stood staring—at Colette then he strode across the space between them and took her in his arms. "Is that what I needed to do to prove my love? This isn't enough?" He bent her back into an embrace that lasted for at least two beats longer than necessary.

When he set her down, Colette's eyes sparkled. "I knew you could never be swayed by someone like Ruby," she said, tossing a glance even smugger than

Mrs. Doon's earlier one in the maid's direction.

"You mean to say you thought he murdered Ruby, but you didn't think him capable of adultery?" Mrs. Doon asked, incredulous.

"Precisely," Colette retorted, never tearing her eyes away from Finn's.

"Oh, lordy lord. You two are meant for one another," Mrs. Doon said, waving her hand at the pair of them in disgust and bustling out of the boudoir.

Chapter Twenty-Two

"Wait." Rosemary spoke up when Colette and Finn made to leave, employing her charms. "Forgive my impertinence, but may I ask a question?"

"I suppose you might as well," Finn said sheepishly, his arm still wrapped securely around Colette's waist, "since you know more about me than you probably ought to after that display."

Rosemary shrugged. "Who amongst us hasn't made a fool of ourselves at one time or another? Call it morbid curiosity, but you said Ruby intended to blackmail you, and if you weren't having an affair with her, what was her ammunition?"

Finn and Colette shared a brief look, then they both shrugged as if making a decision. "She threatened to tell Coco that the Clark family business is nearly bankrupt." That hadn't been what either Rosemary or Imogene expected, but it made sense.

"What she didn't realize is we already knew," Colette

explained. "Hence, my fear about the marriage of convenience. With Pennington Pharmaceuticals at its back, Clark Paper will shift their production to medical products. We'll all be so rich we won't be able to stand it. But I couldn't care less, even if it doesn't pan out. It wouldn't matter to me if you were flat broke. I've got plenty of money." Colette gazed at Finn adoringly. For the first time, there was a sense of calm about her.

"That's right, darling. As long as we're together, that's all that matters. But, there's still a murderer on our hands, and—wait a second," Finn said, taking one step back and raising an eyebrow. "Did you believe I tried to poison your father?"

"Of course not." Colette's brows knit together. "Honestly, I hadn't thought much about it. I assumed Ruby had drunk from the tequila bottle."

"No, the tequila was delivered just yesterday," Imogene explained, for once not earning herself a scathing glare simply for speaking. If it had been a less serious situation, Rosemary might have been amused, wondering what was going through her mind now that Colette and Finn had been cleared as suspects.

"I know I've said a lot of things about my father, but—"

"—he's still your father, and he might be in danger," Finn finished for Colette. "But why? And from whom?"

"Well, the *why* isn't difficult to ascertain," Colette

said. "We aren't the only people he's caused harm to, after all. For all I know, there could be disgruntled burlesque dancers all over downtown. But as much as I'd like to believe it's a stranger, it seems highly unlikely. The killer has to be someone in this house. Leo, perhaps?"

"I hate to say it, but out of all the options, he would be my preference," Finn replied. Leo as the murderer *would* be cleaner for the Penningtons. Nice and neat. "And she *was* propositioning him. I saw it with my own two eyes."

Colette snorted. "You don't have to convince me—that Ruby came on to Leo *or* that he killed her to keep his job. Leo worships my father like he was his own."

Rosemary's heart skipped a beat as a new possibility occurred to her, and a glance at Imogene let her know they had both come to the same conclusion. Finn noticed the look that passed between them and wasn't one to let such a thing pass.

"What?" he asked.

Imogene ignored him, her gaze trained instead on Rosemary. "Perhaps that's why they started sleeping in separate bedrooms," she said excitedly. "It's a wild leap, but…"

Rosemary nodded. "Their ages seem to fit—and didn't Mrs. Doon say that Mrs. Pennington had difficulty carrying her children."

"It wouldn't be an enormous shock. She did have a few years on him, and he wouldn't be the first man to lack patience while waiting for his wife to heal. As if that's the worst part about childbearing—the inconvenience." Imogene huffed.

"Leo might be angry, if that's the case, not to be recognized by the man he idolizes."

"What are the two of you going on about?" Finn interrupted, his voice raised an octave in frustration.

Rosemary sighed and turned to Colette, "Did your mother's diary happen to include dates?"

Colette's mouth opened, and she sucked in a breath, a look of hope on her face that crumpled just as quickly as she realized the answer. "No, no, it didn't. Why?"

"What if Leo really is your father's long-lost son?" Colette turned ashen, and Finn screwed his mouth into a distasteful grimace. "He would have reason to grind an ax if that's the case."

Colette shook her head as if to dislodge the unpleasant thought. "Everyone, please say a prayer it isn't so. And no, there were no dates. I assumed it was recent since the diary was in her closet and not with the rest of them."

"The rest of them?" Imogene's eyes narrowed.

"Mother kept all kinds of diaries in a locked commode in her bedroom. I never thought to read any of them, and

I didn't notice it the last time I was in there. Perhaps you ought to ask Miss Langley." Colette's eyes clouded over. "I'm afraid I might have been too hard on her. Oscar, too. He'll be all I've got left if this madman succeeds!" She buried her face in Finn's chest.

"It's all right, Coco. You'll have me, and we'll do everything we can to protect your father. Oscar will forgive you for being hard on him, you'll see. Perhaps swallow that pride and tell him how you really feel. Now, let's get out of here. I'm taking you to lunch, and we won't return until the auction horde has cleared out." Finn led her towards the door and said, "It seems you two have everything under control. Find out who did this, won't you?"

When they'd gone, and Imogene and Rosemary were alone in Mrs. Pennington's sitting room, they each sank onto an armchair and spent a moment in silent contemplation.

"This whole thing is turning out even more sordid than I could have imagined," Imogene said.

"Words cannot express the truth of that statement," Rosemary replied. "We need those diaries."

"We do." Imogene glanced at the clock on the wall. "There's just enough time before the auction is to begin; let's find Pippa."

Imogene followed Rosemary into the corridor towards the staircase, but before they reached the landing, a noise wafted from the library. "This must be some kind of joke," Imogene said before striding across the parquet and peeking through the crack in the doors.

Inside, Mr. Pennington wandered over the ornamental rug where Ruby had died, the eternal glass of whisky in hand, muttering to himself and occasionally raising his voice to shout something unintelligible. "He's drunk again."

Rosemary took a look and sighed. "We don't have time to deal with him, and really, how is this any different from any other—" Her comment was interrupted when Mr. Pennington noticed he was being observed and strode over to the library doors.

"What are you doing out there, anyway?" he slurred. "Spying on me? Like a couple a…like a couple a…" Whatever it was he wanted to accuse Rosemary and Imogene of resembling was lost as Mr. Pennington descended further into his drunken state.

The overpowering scent of sandalwood permeated the library. "What is that cologne you're wearing?" Rosemary asked, wondering if Mr. Pennington had his cologne imported along with his tequila. The scent conjured images of Ruby's corpse sprawled across the carpet, and Rosemary remembered how she had faintly smelled of Mr. Pennington the day she died. She also noticed one of the swords missing from the wall and hoped he hadn't been playing with it in his inebriated state. Whoever wanted Mr. Pennington dead might not have to try again if he ran himself through.

He took a sniff as if he didn't realize he was as potent as a skunk, and his eyes filled with sorrow. "Ruby used to put it on. She…she said she wanted…wanted to smell like me."

Under normal circumstances, Rosemary might have felt some sympathy for Mr. Pennington, but she was too busy processing his statement. "Ruby used to put on your cologne."

Rosemary stood stock still for a long moment, allowing the implications to sink in. The image of the puncture wound on Ruby's neck scrolled across her mind to the soundtrack of Oscar's declaration after Desmond had been poisoned: *Desmond was lucky the atropine hadn't been introduced directly into his bloodstream.*

Out of Mr. Pennington's earshot, she explained her theory to Imogene. "Ruby spritzed herself with his cologne after they…did whatever it was they were doing," she shivered in disgust, "and Colette was right. She returned to move the Lanvin and got poked with the dressmaking pin."

Imogene let out a groan, having followed the line of thinking to its inevitable end. "The atropine entered her bloodstream, and that was it. The cologne alone wasn't enough to kill her—if it were, he'd be a goner by now."

226

She jerked a thumb in Mr. Pennington's direction.

Oblivious, he continued to blather. "It's ironic, isn't it? Ruby loved that cologne. I suppose it was some small mercy. I never told her it was a gift from Jade." He dissolved into sobs again.

"We'd better go and find Pippa," Rosemary said, but Imogene had stopped in her tracks.

"Wait. You don't think—" Imogene's expression twisted painfully. She had come to a revelation of her own. "You don't think Jade could have before she died—?" She trailed off.

Rosemary's eyes snapped to Mr. Pennington. "Is it possible? For a daily dose of atropine applied topically to be fatal? How long would it take? Or, more importantly, how much would it take?"

Mr. Pennington appeared confused. He shook his head and waved his empty glass around. "You'll have to ask Oscar. He's the one who understands the science behind Pennington Phar...Pharma...ceuticals." He hiccuped and slumped over on the settee with his eyes closed. For a moment, Rosemary thought perhaps the effects of the cologne had overtaken him or that there had been another dose of Bella-quil in his whisky, but when she tentatively pressed her wrist to his forehead, he felt cool as a cucumber.

"He's just passed out. Best to let him sleep it off," she said, leading Imogene from the room and closing the door behind her. "I suppose that answers the question of who the intended victim was."

"I only hope we didn't just answer the question of who tried to bump Mr. Pennington off in the first place."

"Although," Rosemary said slowly, "If Jade did put the poison in his cologne, it still doesn't explain who dosed the tequila and—oh! What if Oscar knew the cologne had been dosed? He *knows the science,* after all, doesn't he? And, if I smelled it on her during the discovery of Ruby's body, he must also have, but he didn't say a word. Perhaps Oscar is more his mother's son than his father's."

Imogene considered. "You think he wanted to avenge her death—or at least put a stop to his father's treachery? Wouldn't *that* be ironic, considering Jade's worries over Oscar turning out like Mr. Pennington? I never thought I'd speak this sentence, but I would prefer it if our first theory was correct and Leo is Mr. Pennington's unbalanced, disgruntled, illegitimate son."

"We need those diaries."

Nodding her agreement, Imogene led the way to the second floor just as the start of the auction was announced, only to discover that Pippa was nowhere to be found. "Drat, she's already gone into the ballroom. We can't interrupt her during the auction, but maybe I can get her attention."

As Rosemary made to follow Imogene across the

portrait gallery to the ballroom's side entrance, she glanced at the wall full of family paintings and photographs. It was as if a cold wind had blown through, and the hairs on the back of Rosemary's neck stood to attention. She squinted at a photograph of Jade wearing a maternity gown, unable to shake the feeling that there was something *off* about it. Finally, she gave in to the niggling sense of imbalance she most often experienced when something in one of her sketches felt out of proportion.

Curious, Imogene stepped up to join her. "What is it?"

Rosemary pointed to the gentle curve at the front of the dress. "Does this look right to you?"

Imogene shrugged. "I suppose so."

But Rosemary was already shaking her head. "It's off. I wouldn't have noticed if not for Vera's little performance with the bum roll today. Look closely and tell me Jade's belly doesn't look exactly like Vera's did earlier."

Imogene did, and she couldn't. Mystified, she asked, "Why would she pretend to be with child? I can't think of a reason."

Rosemary could think of several, but only one made sense to her.

"We know Jade didn't have an easy time carrying Colette. What if she *couldn't* have another baby after that?"

The lack of sleep made Imogene a bit slow to catch on. "Ludicrous. What good would it do to pretend? There still wouldn't be a baby at the end of it. Unless she'd gone cuckoo and only thought she was with child."

"That's one possibility, but I think there's another." The scenario rolled around in Rosemary's head. Not all of the pieces fell neatly into place, but there were enough of them that did to make her think she was close to a breakthrough. "Oscar."

Head shaking, Imogene began to protest, "But that's…" she paused, wrinkled her brow as she puzzled it through, then said, "diabolical, and yet, I think you're right. I wouldn't have said it was possible when Jade was alive, but with what I've learned about her the past couple of days, I've changed my mind."

"That would be a tough pill for anyone to swallow. If Oscar found out, it might have caused him to go a bit barmy. And who could blame him? We need to see those diaries. Now, more than ever. Do you think Pippa's still in the ballroom?" Turning to head in that direction, Rosemary nearly ran down one of the younger maids but couldn't remember her name.

"I'm sorry, miss."

Rosemary waved the apology away. "Have you seen Pippa Langley in the last few minutes? Do you know where she might be?"

"No, miss. I've been sent to look for her, but it's, well, you see, I saw her speaking to Mr. Pennington, and he looked upset."

Dread settled in the pit of Rosemary's stomach.

"She's not with Mr. Pennington, we've just left him in the library, and he was quite alone."

But the maid was shaking her head. "Mr. Pennington, the younger."

CHAPTER TWENTY-THREE

Could Pippa have discovered Oscar's secret? Rosemary didn't dare to ask the question out loud, and she needn't have because it was the thought weighing on Imogene's mind as well. That, and how far he might go to keep her quiet.

She flew down the stairs to the first floor behind Imogene, who tossed over her shoulder, "You check the smoking room and the salon. I'll take the morning room and see if any of the kitchen staff have seen her."

Pippa wasn't in the salon, and while Rosemary didn't expect to find her in Mr. Pennington's smoking room, she took a cursory glance anyway. Quite a few auction guests had broken away from the ballroom to shamelessly peruse the rest of the mansion. A pair of cagey-looking men were busy ogling the baseball memorabilia, and before she had time to think, Rosemary cried, "Hey, what do you think you're doing in here?"

The men turned and appraised her disheveled appearance. "You don't look like you own the place," one of them said snidely. Deliberately, he picked up the baseball, tossed it in the air, and caught it again, his eyes never leaving Rosemary's in a challenge.

Without warning, she opened her mouth and let out a scream that on any other day might have drawn half the household, but with all the hullabaloo only served to surprise the two men and summon one confused-looking maid from the corridor. "May I help you?"

"Have you seen Pippa Langley? Or Oscar Pennington?" Rosemary demanded. Wide-eyed, the maid shook her head, causing Rosemary to let out a frustrated expletive. She turned to go, tossing over her shoulder in a fair imitation of Imogene, "And you might want to eighty-six these boobs before Mr. Pennington discovers they've been rifling through his things and sends them out of here in a meat wagon."

Satisfied, she smiled, but it was quickly replaced with a frown that only deepened when she converged with Imogene at the foot of the staircase. "Nobody's seen either of them." They quickened their pace and ascended to the second floor, doing one more cursory search of the ballroom and portrait gallery before arriving on the third-level landing.

The doors to the library were still closed, just as they'd left them, but Imogene cracked one open and peeked inside. "Empty. Mr. Pennington must have found his second wind. Hopefully, he went to his bed to sleep it off."

With Colette gone, all of the family bedrooms were quiet, Jade's wardrobe a shadow of its former self. By the time they reached the guest suites, Imogene had worked herself into an utter panic. "Where could they be?" She practically flew down the corridor towards Desmond's room.

Frederick had been sitting at Desmond's bedside, but when Rosemary and Imogene came crashing through the door, he jumped to attention, brandishing Mr. Pennington's missing sword, and let out a roar.

For a split second, everybody froze, and then Desmond let out a scratchy-sounding chuckle.

"What on earth are you doing with that thing?" Rosemary demanded of Frederick.

"What does it look like I'm doing? I'm protecting Desmond, of course."

"From the maids? I'm surprised they'll bring your trays in, you acting like that. Although, I'd advise against eating or drinking anything prepared within these walls, anyway. Have you seen Pippa?" It all came out in a rush, and Frederick grew concerned.

"Pippa? No, why?"

"She's in danger, that's why," Rosemary said. "Stay here, watch Des, and if Oscar comes around, keep your guard up. But you'll have to find another weapon because I'm taking this." She divested Frederick of the sword and herded Imogene out the door before her brother could pick his jaw up off the floor. "Where would you go if you didn't want to be found?" Rosemary asked on the way back towards the stairs.

"Oh, for crying out loud." Imogene took a sharp left and came to a stop outside the library doors. "The secret speakeasy room. It's the only place that makes sense."

Rosemary nodded and followed Imogene into the library, sword in hand. When her eyes landed on the spot where its twin had been displayed and discovered an empty stretch of wall, she tightened her grip. "Should we go and get help?" she whispered.

"It could be too late by then," Imogene replied. "Drat! If only I hadn't worn these shoes and left my pistol at the Red Door."

The sound of a garbled moan—Pippa, to be certain—interrupted the debate and sent adrenaline coursing through Rosemary's veins.

"Don't worry," she said, waving the sword. "Fred taught me a thing or two, and we know Oscar doesn't have any skill when it comes to fencing." She approached the hidden panel behind the fireplace, moved into an offensive stance, then locked eyes with Imogene and nodded sharply once.

At the signal, Imogene threw open the panel to reveal

what looked like a scene from one of Vera's outlandish plays. Pippa sat slumped, nearly unconscious, in one of the leather armchairs in the center of the room, her wrists and ankles bound to the arms and feet of the chair, a gag in her mouth. Her blouse had been ripped open, its buttons scattered to the floor.

That alone was enough to send any sane person screaming back out through the door, but it still wasn't the most surprising thing in the room. Mr. Pennington—sans trousers—lay sprawled on the pile carpet. The sight of his sock garters made Rosemary shudder in distaste. He still reeked of sandalwood but looked no worse than when they'd left him in the library earlier.

And still, the real shock was that their captor wasn't Oscar Pennington—it was Mrs. Doon!

"What in holy hell?" Imogene exclaimed as the maid spun around from whatever she'd been fiddling with on one of the shelves. Her eyes flicked from the sword in Rosemary's hand to the one leaning against the coffee table a few feet to her right. "I wouldn't," Imogene warned.

Rosemary took a step forward, but Mrs. Doon held up a hand. "And *you* shouldn't. If you get any closer, I won't tell you how they were dosed, and your hopes of saving them will be dashed." Rosemary stopped in her tracks, and for a long moment, she and Imogene stood staring at one another, uncertain whether Mrs. Doon was telling the truth. When they silently agreed to err on the side of caution, the maid smiled and said, "Close the door and drop the weapon."

Imogene did as she was bid while Rosemary hesitantly lowered the sword, taking a couple of steps backward and holding her hands up in surrender.

Mrs. Doon nodded once and took a step closer to her own weapon but didn't reach for it. "He deserves what's coming to him, you know."

"And what about Pippa?" Imogene asked, to which Mrs. Doon merely gestured towards Mr. Pennington's prone figure. "Surely you aren't suggesting the two of them—? Why that's ludicrous!"

Mrs. Doon's expression turned hard. "Nobody is innocent, Miss Quinn. You, of all people, ought to know that." She scowled, and as she became distracted by whatever demons whispered in her ear, Rosemary and Imogene shared a confused glance.

They were missing something, like the puzzles on the wall at the Red Door, the one illuminating fact that would make all the other pieces form a picture. It felt like the answer was on the tip of Rosemary's tongue, but Mrs. Doon had begun to twitter, wringing her hands and muttering under her breath. "Miss Langley should have minded her station. It wasn't any of her nevermind, was it?"

A feeling of dread built in Rosemary's stomach as though she'd been delivered a knockout punch, and the solution to the mystery came zinging into focus with perfect clarity.

How many times had she heard that phrase, *none of my nevermind*, since arriving in the Pennington mansion? Mrs. Doon used it habitually, but she wasn't the only one. Oscar had said it as well, his inflection similar enough to Mrs. Doon to spark a realization that seemed so far-fetched Rosemary could hardly believe it. And yet, there was no other explanation that fit so neatly.

Mrs. Doon had been the one to mention Jade expecting Colette Colette, but according to Mrs. Russel, Mrs. Doon hadn't been working at the mansion when she started—*shortly before Oscar was born*. Oscar, who, now that Rosemary was paying attention, bore a hint of resemblance to Mrs. Doon. Perhaps more than a hint.

"So you're going to murder Pippa, just like you murdered Ruby?" Imogene asked before Rosemary could catch her breath to comment. "Why?"

With a scowl, Mrs. Doon shook her head. "No, no, no. That's where you've got it all wrong. Ruby wasn't supposed to die. Only Charles. He's the one who deserved to pay for his sins."

"Then why aren't you responsible for yours?" Oscar's voice cut through the brief silence that had followed

Mrs. Doon's declaration, and he stepped into the little room behind the fireplace wearing an unfathomable expression—one that mirrored his mother's so perfectly Imogene gasped. She and Rosemary locked eyes, and Rosemary nodded once.

Oscar's gaze landed on Pippa and his face contorted with rage. "What did you do to her?"

"Nothing," Mrs. Doon squeaked. "Just a little dose. It will all be all right, you'll see. I'll keep my boy with me, and everything will be perfect now, won't it?"

"I don't know what you imagine you mean to me," Oscar spat, "but I'm not your boy, and if you think I'm going to let you hurt either of them—"

Mrs. Doon lunged for the sword and, given it was an unexpected move, managed to get it into her hands and to Mr. Pennington's chest before Oscar could stop her. "Don't move, or I'll cut him, and he's already doused with that cologne he loves so much. We both know what will happen if I do—the same thing that happened to Ruby."

Oscar stepped back and squared his shoulders, his eyes smoldering. "Why do you need to do this now? Why not years ago? In fact, why did you agree to it at all in the first place?"

"Why, so you would have a better life than I could ever give you, of course," Mrs. Doon said as if it should be obvious.

Rosemary had already put most of the pieces together, so while Mrs. Doon appealed to her son, she appraised the room for some way out of the debacle she and Imogene had found themselves in.

"I was hardly more than a girl when I started here, and I didn't know what to expect—certainly not to develop a flirtation with the man of the house. I had no idea it was just a dalliance for him, and it didn't take long to realize it was all a mistake. I broke it off, but then I found out—I found out I was going to have you."

Mrs. Doon's eyes turned misty as she thought about the past, but Oscar's remained trained on Pippa. When Rosemary followed his gaze and saw that she had begun to stir, her heart skipped a beat. If Pippa fully roused and found herself tied to a chair, she likely wouldn't remain silent, and Rosemary didn't want to find out how Mrs. Doon might react.

"I went to Mrs. Pennington and confessed everything. She already suspected, of course. Nothing got by her. But she didn't know about the baby. She told me your sister's birth had rendered her unable to have more children and that Mr. Pennington desperately wanted a son."

Oscar's jaw clenched, but he listened to the sordid story of his conception and the deception that followed without speaking.

"She offered to raise you herself as Mr. Pennington's

legitimate son. It was more than I could ever do for you, but I couldn't bear to leave you, so I begged her to let me stay on. She took mercy on me and gave me the gift of watching you grow into the fine young man you've become. I went away, and Jade pretended to be expecting a child. She used the affair as an excuse to banish Mr. Pennington from her rooms, and he never caught on. When I returned, we decided I would become Mrs. Doon to keep him from wanting to continue the affair. For all his faults, your father doesn't chase after married women."

Rosemary sensed Mrs. Doon was winding down, and behind her, Pippa was beginning to wake up. The moment hung heavy, and she felt as though she needed to *do* something but didn't know what. Her eyes flicked to the sword and then to Imogene, and another unspoken understanding passed between them.

"That wasn't the only secret she kept," Imogene said, catching Mrs. Doon's attention. "The truth is, she hated you. She thought you were getting exactly what you deserved, and she enjoyed watching you have to watch Oscar grow up while denying your connection with him. You were played for a fool."

Imogene's barb hit the mark, and Mrs. Doon's entire face seemed to expand for a moment. Her eyes bugged, her nostrils flared, and she began to shake. "You're lying."

"She's not," Oscar declared. "I found the rest of Mother's diaries. She tolerated you because she loved me. She loved me despite her anger and her bitterness. She wasn't perfect, but she was my mother."

Coming from Oscar, the dismissal was worse than a slap in the face, and it caused Mrs. Doon a split second of pause—just long enough for chaos to erupt. Rosemary lunged for her sword, and Imogene darted for Mrs. Doon, realizing belatedly that their silent conversation should have included Oscar. In a chivalrous maneuver, he tried to put himself between Pippa and the woman who gave birth to him just as Imogene made her move. The two slammed into each other then rebounded in different directions. Oscar stumbled into Mrs. Doon, the pair of them going down in a tangle of limbs.

"Ahh!" Mrs. Doon let out a strangled cry and held up her arm. A line of blood welled from a long but shallow slice across her wrist.

"You'll live," Oscar said, rising to his feet just as Imogene pulled the gag out of Pippa's mouth. "Unless, of course, there are traces of atropine anywhere near that cut."

He turned away as if washing his hands of her, but then his eyes met Pippa's for a long moment, and he seemed to have a change of heart. "Here," he said, pulling a small vial from his trouser pocket. "I don't want to be anything like you. Drink this, and you'll be fine."

That said, he bent to release Pippa from the chair, lifted her into his arms, and laid his lips on hers. Pippa didn't seem to mind.

***

Later that evening, after the doctor had seen to various minor injuries and administered tonics all around, Rosemary and Imogene relayed the events of the afternoon to a stunned household.

"We've been rendered entirely unnecessary again, haven't we, Freddie?"

"Certainly have, Des old boy. That's what happens when you throw in with a couple of capable women." He peered at his friends with admiration. "Though it would be lovely if they'd stop trying to get themselves killed."

"Where would be the fun in that?" Rosemary and Imogene both asked at the same time.

"It would be lovely if I hadn't been left out," Vera pouted.

"But then you wouldn't have been able to buy all those gorgeous dresses, now would you?" Frederick pointed out.

Somewhat mollified, Vera winked at Colette and said,

"I promise to be good to them."

"I've no doubt," Colette replied. "And I promise to be good to my brother from here on out." Her attention shifted to Pippa as if to include her in the vow.

Oscar hadn't moved more than two inches away from Pippa since they'd exited the speakeasy room and watched Mrs. Doon get carted away by the police, and he leaned even closer now. He appeared dumbstruck, and Rosemary suspected it had as much to do with the outpouring of love as it did with the bizarre events of the afternoon.

Finn threw in with Colette, of course, offering Oscar some words of support, and even Imogene swallowed her pride. "I'm truly sorry for having made a series of incorrect assumptions about your integrity," she said, to which Oscar replied with a look of confusion.

"She's never actually disparaged you *to* you," Pippa said, "so that was more an apology for me. Which I appreciate."

Bleary-eyed, Mr. Pennington took Pippa's hand in his own. "You'd be a welcome addition to the family," he said, "no matter what Ruby thought. You have my blessing."

"They don't need your blessing, Father," Colette said, receiving a grateful smile from her brother. "But they'll have mine as well. Father's giving me the house, Oscar, and I'm afraid I'm going to have to insist you find other accommodations. Sign the papers on that apartment you've been dreaming about, and when you're settled, invite Finn and me over for dinner."

"I know I have a lot to make up for," Mr. Pennington said with a sigh. "And I'm prepared to try. Starting with giving up the juice. Say," he said, turning to Desmond and Frederick, "would either of you gentlemen enjoy some imported rum?"

Chapter Twenty-Four

It had been a week since the events at the Pennington mansion, and Rosemary and her friends had done their best to put it all behind them—except for Vera. She would remember every time she looked at any of the pieces she'd purchased from Jade's wardrobe, including the Lanvin, which had been a gift from Colette. Rosemary herself would have preferred to go home with the Mary Cassatt, but it was to be displayed in a place of pride in Oscar's new apartment, right where it belonged.

"We were all wrong this time," Frederick had cheerfully pointed out during the group's last conversation about the murder. "Nobody suspected Mrs. Doon was the murderer—or Oscar's mother. It wasn't only me on the wrong track for once! I just hope he isn't scarred for life by the whole debacle. Discovering your mother isn't really your mother must be quite a shock."

"He has the love of a good woman to help him through," Imogene said. "Pippa will take care of him, and he'll come to terms with it. People aren't always who we think they are, but that doesn't mean we stop caring about them." It seemed as though she had reconciled her own feelings regarding Jade, and with that final conclusion, the subject was dropped.

The remainder of the holiday was spent touring the city: they visited the Statue of Liberty, perused the Metropolitan Museum of Art, and even walked across the Brooklyn Bridge. Frederick convinced Desmond to take in two more baseball games and even managed to score himself a ball signed by his hero, Babe Ruth. Vera dragged Rosemary to a musical and three plays and stripped several Fifth Avenue shops down to their bones. And they ended every evening at the Red Door.

"I can't believe you're leaving tomorrow!" Tuesday bemoaned while pouring gin into a line of teacups. "You'll be back, won't you? Someday?" It was Saturday night, and the speakeasy was hopping, so packed to the gills that Tuesday didn't have a chance to hear Rosemary's response before being bombarded with orders. Imogene had been forced behind the bar alongside her, and there were two bussers Rosemary had never seen before carrying endless tubs of china back and forth.

"At least we're going out with a bang." Rosemary took a deep breath and looked down at her ensemble. She veritably sparkled beneath the twinkling chandeliers in a sheath of beaded satin. Her long hair had been styled into a faux bob held in place with a diamanté-encrusted headband, and her lips were painted crimson. While she might have looked the part, Rosemary didn't consider herself a canary and had vehemently resisted the group's insistence that she sing.

And yet, there she was, preparing to do just that, largely to appease Vera, who she knew was still put out about missing the Pennington action. "It'll be fun, Rosie, a lark," she said, straightening her bodice and checking her lipstick in a hand mirror produced from the depths of her handbag.

"Oh no," Vera said suddenly, her eye caught by something in the mirror. She turned around with narrowed eyes and pointed to a man wearing a coat and tie and a supercilious smile. "That's Isaac Allen, the smarmy film producer from my audition. Don't say anything to Freddie," she hastened to add. "Just get out there and sing your heart out, and then we'll do our little skit."

Her nerves jumping, Rosemary took the microphone, opened her mouth, and let the first notes of "Blue Skies" float into the bar. The place went quiet as she sang. Vera had been right. Performing was fun.

When the song ended, Vera joined Rosemary on the makeshift stage and launched into a parody of an Englishwoman arriving for her first visit to New York and ending up at the Red Door. The crowd went wild when Vera flawlessly mimicked Imogene's accent and personality.

"Hey, darlin', you look familiar. Have we slept together before?" Before they could return to their seats, Isaac Allen approached Vera, forcing Rosemary to swallow the urge to vomit on his Italian leather loafers.

"No, I auditioned for you. And I told you then that I didn't want to sleep with you." Vera's tone was acid. "I'll stick to the stage, where the real actors are, and you can take your film role and—"

Mr. Allen raised his hands in surrender, "Sorry if you took it the wrong way, doll, but that's just the nature of the business. If you want to be a star, you've got to be willing to put in the work." He swiveled his head suggestively and wiggled his eyebrows.

"You're a pig," Vera retorted, "and I suppose it's because you lack the," she matched his condescending tone and manner, "*prowess* to get women into your bed without promises of making them a star."

Mr. Allen's tablemate let out a snort. "Looks like she's got you pegged." He turned to Vera and handed her his card. "If you're interested in a legitimate audition, call me."

"Thank you. But I've realized fame isn't the motivator it once was. I love my life. I love acting, too, but I can do that at home. And I can do it in addition to all the other things I want to do. If that makes me less of a feminist, so be it. But isn't the point of being able to do what we want actually being able to do *what we want*?"

"Yes," Rosemary and Imogene both said at once. "It is."

Later, after he'd gone, Vera asked, "Would it be unfeminist of me to wish Freddie *had* given him a fat lip?"

It was just Rosemary who replied this time. "Oh, don't worry, he still got what was coming to him. I served him a sneezer."

Britsh English

Barmy - a crazy idea

   Block of flats - apartment building

   Bloody - an intensifying mild expletive (swear word)

   Bollocks - dismay or disbelief

   Car park - parking lot

   Cheeky - endearingly rude or disrespectful

   Chinwag - a gossip session

   Chuffed - to be very pleased or happy about something

   Cracking - good or excellent; to get started doing something

   Cuppa - cup of (usually tea)

   Daft - a bit stupid or silly

   Diamante – rhinestone

   Dodgy - questionable or suspicious

   Dolt - a fool

   Fancy - a verb expressing desire ("do you fancy some

dinner?")

Footway – sidewalk

Fringe (hair) – bangs

Gobsmacked - shocked

Holiday - vacation

Jumble sale - yard/lawn/garage sale

Loo - the toilet

Lorry - truck

Match - game

Pinch - to steal

Solicitor – lawyer

Stodgy -

Sweets - candy

To nick/to get nicked - to steal/to be arrested for a crime

Trollop - a loose woman; a woman with low morals (derogatory)

Underground - subway

1920's Slang

Bearcat - a fiery woman
Beat it - scram or get lost
Berries - similar to bee's knees, as in "It's the berries."
Blotto - drunk
Blow one down - to kill someone
Boob - a stupid man
Bootleg - illegal liquor
Bum's Rush - ejection by force from an establishment
Bump/bump off - to kill
Canary - a female singer
Cat's meow - great, excellent, outstanding
Chopper squad - guys with machine guns
Copacetic - wonderful, fine, all right
Cups under - drunk
Dumb Dora - a stupid woman
Eighty-six (or 86) - nix or eliminate

Fire extinguisher - a killjoy

Flat tire – a dull, insipid, disappointing person

Gold digger - a woman who associates with or marries a man for his wealth

Goon - a thug

Juice joint - a speakeasy

Meat wagon - an ambulance

Ossified - drunk

Palooka - a man who is not bright

Pill - an unlikable person

Speakeasy – Irish word to describe an illicit, undercover bar selling bootleg liquor

Teetotaler - a person who abstains from the consumption of alcohol

Volsteadian - of or relating to Prohibition

Wet Blanket - a solemn person, a killjoy